'*You're exa*   *day to*
take me hon   an who
stops by l.   b. But
the last thing Ben Maddox, hellbent on   ersonal
vendetta, wants is a woman to tag along with him—
however beautiful or however well she can cook.

Sanna, the eternal optimist, knows that Ben is her
only chance of escape to the better life she dreams of. He
was her man. *She* knew it. Why didn't he?

SILK FOR A LADY

ROSINA PYATT

MILLS & BOON LIMITED
15–16 BROOK'S MEWS
LONDON W1A 1DR

*First published in Great Britain 1984
by Mills & Boon Limited*

© Rosina Pyatt 1984

*Australian copyright 1984
Philippine copyright 1984
This edition 1984*

ISBN 0 263 74915 0

*Set in 10 on 12 pt Linotron Times
04-1184-60,000*

*Photoset by Rowland Phototypesetting Ltd
Bury St Edmunds, Suffolk
Made and printed in Great Britain by
Cox and Wyman Ltd, Reading*

CHAPTER
ONE

'SIT LIKE a woman. Only a boy would spread his legs like that. And cover your hair! You know what to expect if you cause me trouble.' José Vargas spoke in Spanish, his reedy voice at odds with his body. The sheer bulk of it blocked the sunlight from the room as he turned in the open doorway to look out over the scorched earth.

Sanna, sitting cross-legged among the cooking-pans on the earthen floor, rolled her expressive eyes heavenwards and breathed, 'These things are sent to try us, as Mr Blakeney used to say.' For a few seconds she mused on this and other favourite sayings of her old mentor, then she added wistfully, 'What I don't understand, and never shall, is why I have to be tried more than most . . .'

'What nonsense are you muttering, girl?' Vargas growled, turning ponderously to scowl at her.

She didn't answer. She had been made aware with painful frequency that her habit of talking to herself incensed him, and that not replying when spoken to was worse, and usually she was cautious. Today, however, the perverse imp of mischief within her, which refused to lie dormant for long, chose to bubble up and goad Vargas to wrath by letting the silence linger.

He reacted as if his very manhood were at stake, for

she was only a female and could not be allowed to question his authority, even mutely. 'Speak to me if you have something to say, otherwise keep your mouth shut,' he howled, 'and do as I ordered. Sit decently!'

'Better a living dog than a dead lion', quoted Sanna's unrepentant imp, as she matched philosophy to action by obediently uncrossing her legs, tucking them to one side and draping her long black skirt modestly over them.

Vargas, however, was in a volatile mood and did not choose to be appeased. 'Cover your head. How many times do I have to tell you?' he raged.

The imp of mischief, its damage done, subsided, leaving a frightened Sanna to extricate herself from a dangerous situation as hastily as she could. She looked at her hands, dirty from working on the fire, and with careful fingertips lifted her black shawl from her shoulders to hide her bright hair. She liked to be clean, even when trembling with dread. It was her way of showing she was different, that in spite of everything she still clung to hope.

This stubbornness was tempered by the sunny nature of a born optimist and when Vargas, after regarding her for several fulminating moments, once more turned his back on her she quickly recovered from her fright. Deep within her was the unshakable conviction that if she seized her chance when it came, this phase of her life would end as abruptly as all the rest.

In the meantime she had her memories to sustain her. They were jumbled, and sometimes fact was blurred by fantasy where she had mulled over them so long, yet still they shone like beacons through her drab existence to remind her of the land she came from and had to get back to.

Memories of great white houses, and grass so green that she blinked as she recalled it, and marvelled anew that it was grown for prettiness and not for goats to eat. Most of all she remembered pale ladies in rustling dresses who were so pampered by their gentlemen they were allowed to throw silk cushions on the grass to sit on.

This was the greatest wonder of all to Sanna, who wore threadbare cotton and lived in a world where women were less than nothing. It was why she had to get out of Mexico and back to the United States. She belonged among those fine ladies. She knew it as surely as she knew her own name. Better, really, because she didn't have a proper name at all.

She had heard that the Civil War between the northern and southern States, which had actually been the beginning of all her troubles, was over now—and though she understood war wasn't kind, she didn't think it could be cruel enough to wipe away all she remembered.

Indeed, her greatest worry about her return to her own kind was whether she could actually bring herself to throw a silk cushion on to grass, where it might get stained and dirty. She didn't know how she was going to bring herself to be careless with something so precious, but she would have to learn, or she would never be truly a lady.

Sanna, dreaming her muddled but marvellous dreams, leaned forward to blow fresh life into the fire. She blew until she was light-headed, and flames flickered to kindle the twigs she placed across the near-dead embers. She heaped more wood on top and fussed the pieces this way and that until she was satisfied she would soon be able to cook.

She sat back and saw pictures in the flames that had nothing to do with the hovel she found herself in during the Mexican summer of 1867. She jumped when Vargas glanced back at her and snapped, 'Move yourself, girl. He will soon be here.'

Sanna stood up. Her movements were like that of a young colt still learning to co-ordinate growing limbs, one moment all awkwardness and the next unbelievably graceful.

Real beauty was beginning to distinguish the childhood prettiness of her face, for her features were emerging from the blurring plumpness of adolescence. Her figure, similarly, was whittling into shapely well-defined lines. It was her colouring, however, that made her a rarity on this side of the border. Her fair hair and skin had forced Vargas to pay a high price for her.

Sanna was aware that when her chance to escape came she had nothing but herself to trade with. She had a firm picture of the man she would offer herself to in exchange for a safe passage over the border. He would be fair-haired and blue-eyed like herself, strong enough to take her away from Vargas, and young and slim enough not to be repulsive.

She wouldn't let herself despair of ever meeting such a man, though time was running short and the fear that Vargas's son would arrive first was increasing daily. She had never met Eduardo, the man she had been bought for.

Her knowledge of what was happening in the world was slight, and gleaned from listening to Vargas and his wife talk. From them she had learned that the French had occupied Mexico and that Eduardo had gone south to join the patriot Benito Juárez in fighting them.

Only this week a man travelling up from Mexico City had brought news of Eduardo, and it had been bad for Sanna. The French were defeated, and Eduardo, hopefully with plunder, was expected home at any time—and Sanna was the prize selected to keep him there.

She tried to picture a young Vargas, but the reality of his father was too nauseating. Everything about him sagged, as though needing support to prevent him from disintegrating into one great globule of fat. Eye-pouches rested on puffy cheeks, cheeks on chins, chins on chest, and chest on stomach.

Sanna, with all the fastidiousness and idealism of youth, thought him horrible and couldn't imagine his son any less so. When she had been ordered away from her usual chores to cook for an approaching horseman, she had been seized with dread. Yet if it was Eduardo returning, Vargas was showing no signs of joy, and surely he would have recognised his own son by now?

As the minutes passed quietly, her dread lessened and her natural buoyancy reasserted itself. Once more she was able to brush aside the horror of living out her life in this miserable collection of huts that made up Vargas's trading-post at the foothills to a pass through the Sierra Madre mountains.

The buildings were so low they looked as if they had given up the struggle to raise themselves out of the sand. The sun-dried mud bricks had never been plastered or whitewashed, and Sanna waged a daily war to keep this main room free of sand and dirt and straying chickens.

There was nothing to help her make the room cheerful. The walls and ceiling were blackened by smoke from the fire, and Vargas kept the two tiny windows shuttered against the sun. The only furnishings were benches on either side of a long wooden table and a few shelves cluttered with bottles. No pictures, even the customary religious ones, brightened the walls, and the curtained archway at the back of the room led to equally depressing private quarters.

The dreary place had never seemed like home to Sanna, although she had known worse and was willing to risk anything to get away from it. A chance, however slight, was her constant prayer and one she fully expected to be granted. She was owed it, therefore it would come.

Vargas was fidgeting in the doorway. He knew she needed to pass him to wash her hands and fetch fresh water before she cooked. He wouldn't get out of the way. Bitter experience had taught Sanna that he was waiting for her to push past him.

He was anticipating the excitement of her body touching his, however briefly. It puzzled Sanna how even her revulsion stimulated him. Although his back was towards her she knew his eyes were glistening like ripe olives in their fleshy pouches, that he was sucking his drooping moustache, and that the smell of fresh lust was mingling with the rancid odour of his unwashed body.

He had owned her for two years and desired her all that time. At first she had been scared of him, then she'd learned that one scream from her would bring his vicious little wife running to her rescue. Señora Vargas was dead to the world at the moment, sunk in one of her periodic alcoholic stupors, but Sanna didn't think Vargas would bother her much with a customer coming in.

She moved stealthily forward, then made a rush to squeeze round the door frame, keeping her back to him.

He pushed his body sideways to trap her but she was quick and agile enough to get through.

His exertion had been slight but his frustration was great, and Vargas was breathing heavily as he snarled, 'I could make life so much easier for you if you were nice to me, only you are too stupid to realise it.'

'If every fool wore a crown, most of us would be kings,' Sanna retorted, daring to be cheeky again now that she was in the open.

Vargas's fists clenched. 'I am sick of you and your silly sayings. Eduardo will teach you to speak sense when he comes home.'

But Sanna had pulled her shawl forward to protect her face from the fierce sun and was walking away from him to the well, which provided good water all the year round. The spring rains that had swollen the stream flowing from the mountains were little more than a forgotten memory, and only the livestock drank its shallow warm water.

Sanna's nose wrinkled at the stench from a near-by pen where, under a makeshift roof supported by sun-bleached poles, pigs snuffled and snorted. Scrawny chickens scratched, fluttered and fought among them.

Beyond the pens, flies swarmed above a larger enclosure where horses, donkeys and goats grazed listlessly. On the other side of the stream, maize, beans and sunflowers grew in haphazardly cultivated patches. There was nothing else but sand dotted with scrubs distorted into strange shapes by their search for water. Finally, like an act of mercy, mountains rose to limit the desolate scene.

The land looked as though the horn of plenty had been emptied of everything worth having before it was created, so that only the rock-bottom dregs of life were left to sprinkle over the sand. The sparse vegetation was thorned or spiked. The loathsome creatures that crawled or flew were armed with bites or stings, and Sanna was watching for them as she drew up a bucketful of water.

She tipped some into a bowl and washed her hands and face, darting quick glances across the wasteland to see what kind of a man was riding in. Vargas was staring at her, and would be swift to pounce if she showed too much interest.

Honest travellers were few and far between, and she usually had to hide in her room when there were customers, for Vargas feared she would be stolen from him. Only occasionally, with his wife drunk and just one visitor, would she be brought out to cook.

Today, then, might offer the chance she had been praying for. She was tingling with hope as she dabbed her face with her shawl and shook her hands in the sun to dry them, though there was little yet to justify it. The haze rising from the scorched earth caused the outlines of two horses and one man to shimmer, denying her any details, no matter how hard she squinted.

'Take the goods the gods provide,' Sanna advised herself out loud. 'That's what Mr Blakeney would say right now, or would it be the one about "out of the cooking-pan into the fire"? That's the trouble with sayings, there's always another one that says the opposite.'

She raised her eyes from the shimmering horses to the cloudless sky. 'I don't know why I miss you, Mr Blakeney, because you never cared much about me, but I do, and that's a fact. Would you be missing me, I wonder, if I had died and you had lived?'

The sky offered no answer, but Vargas shouted, 'Get about your cooking. He will soon be here.'

Sanna picked up the bucket of water and walked towards him. He was ready for her, and his body seemed to expand in the doorway, filling the space she had to squeeze through.

'Move out of the way or I'll scream,' Sanna told him. She pointed over her shoulder at the rider. 'If I don't wake your wife, that man might do something about it.'

Uncertainty flickered in Vargas's eyes as he looked from her to his customer. Like most bullies, he took no chances with the unknown. He moved out of the doorway, but threatened, 'Keep your hair hidden and your head bowed when you serve him. If you speak, it will be days before you speak again.'

He watched her broodingly as she resumed her place by the fire, and licked his lips as he imagined his son taming her. Eduardo was a good boy. He would share her when she was too cowed to care or complain any more.

He sighed, wishing it were his son coming now, yet, even with the haze, he knew that this man rode differently. When he turned his back on Sanna and stared out again, the shapes had ceased to shimmer and his uncertainty deepened into unease.

There seemed something inexorable about the steady pace at which the man approached the trading-store. Vargas had the uncanny feeling he was capable of riding right through it if he wished, and that the bricks would crumble away to allow his passage.

It was superstitious nonsense to think such things, yet Vargas crossed himself quickly and breathed a few words to his patron saint. If this was the man he had been warned to expect . . .

His nebulous fears increased to panic proportions. He wished he had tried to rouse his wife and hidden the girl. It was too late now. The man was here and there was nothing in his size or face to offer reassurance.

Vargas moved forward and the sudden rush of sunlight from the empty doorway made Sanna blink. She looked round and saw Vargas bobbing and bowing with the cringing servitude that came upon him only when he was extremely frightened.

She left her cooking and crept to the door. As she peeped out, the single braid into which she had plaited her long thick hair felt heavy on her neck. The man was dismounting and his face was hidden to her.

Acute disappointment almost made her gasp, for he was wearing the trousers tight at the thighs and embroidered at the seams that Mexicans favoured, together with a dark poncho. Then she saw his hat had the wide curly brim that Americans wore, and she dared to hope again.

He towered above the fawning Vargas, and there was something about the straight-backed discipline with which he stood and moved that touched a chord in Sanna's memory. She quivered with concentration as her mind jumped from one episode to another in her chaotic past to trace the stamp that this man bore.

Then it came to her. He was a soldier. She had seen many of them clothed in fine grey uniforms when the war had started, the civil one between the States that had resulted in her violent exile.

Sanna desperately wanted to see his face. Those uniformed men were all wrapped up in her mind with the ladies in fine dresses who curled their hair, wore dainty shoes, twirled frilly parasols and sat on silk cushions.

Her even white teeth bit into her full lower lip as she willed him to look her way, and her pulses jumped as he took off his hat and wiped his forehead with the back of his hand. His short hair was light brown, sun-bleached in parts, totally different from Vargas's greasy black locks.

Abruptly, as if conscious of her scrutiny, he swung her way. His face was covered in stubble and dust so that she could see little of his features. She had a swift impression of lean hardness, but what parted her lips in a soft 'Oh' of joy was the blue of the eyes burning into her own.

So many bad things had happened to Sanna that she could no longer cry with sadness. She faced adversity dry-eyed, the hurt intensifying because it had no relief in tears. It was happiness she couldn't cope with, and it spilled out of her eyes like a dam released. Tears trickled down her cheeks, chased by more. He had come at last. A man she could accept.

He was staring at her as incredulously as she stared at him, and for Sanna it meant that her long exile was over. She was beautiful and he would want her. That was the way of men, or why else would Vargas take such pains to keep her hidden? How ironic that, the one time it really mattered, she had not been shut up.

It was long seconds before she realised that Vargas was also staring at her, and scowling. Habit rather than fear made her retreat into the room. The man—her man—was strong enough to take her away from here. She had nothing more to worry about.

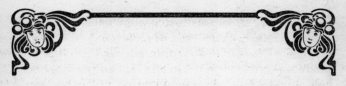

CHAPTER
TWO

WHILE SANNA'S excitement rose to fever pitch inside the house, Ben Maddox was leading his horses to the stream, his lean features expressionless, no trace remaining of his surprise at seeing a beautiful girl weeping and staring at him as though he were the crock of gold at the end of the rainbow.

It was true she had shocked him out of his habitual indifference, but only for a moment. The illusion that he was looking at Clare had lasted no longer. It was the colouring that had tricked him. The face, of course, had to be different.

And so his interest in her died; whatever had caused her to stare and cry like that, it was no business of his. A girl with hair the colour of ripened corn and eyes as blue as a mountain lake had to be stolen, but that was common enough, and beyond wondering how many times she had been bartered before arriving here in the middle of nowhere, he had no difficulty dismissing her from his mind.

Circumstances had made him as savage and unfeeling as the land he found himself in, and so he was equal to it. In that respect, Sanna's instinct hadn't been wrong. He was precisely the kind of man she needed to get her safely away. It was merely her misfortune that of all creatures on earth he distrusted women most.

Luisa, Linda, Clare—the women who had helped to shape him—had all in their different ways betrayed him. There was no softness left in him for Sanna. She needed him, but to Ben she amounted to no more than a distraction, and he wasn't a man who allowed himself to be distracted. It was his single-mindedness that had enabled him to get this far, and it would get him home again.

Home . . . Ben savoured the word experimentally like a forgotten taste. The great *estancia*, or estate, which his father had secured through marriage, had changed little since its thousands of acres had been granted by the king of Spain to those of his stepmother's ancestors who had followed the *conquistadores* into New Mexico and settled there.

By later conquest, and by purchase, New Mexico now belonged to the United States, which put the *estancia* firmly on the right side of the border with Mexico, as far as the Maddox family was concerned. They called it a ranch and anglicised its name to Blue Tree Valley, but much of its old, almost feudal, order still remained. So, too, did its jewel of a *hacienda*, its sweet green grass and its protective mountains clothed in the spruces which had given the valley its name.

Ben checked his reverie. It wasn't a good thing to think of home before he had earned the right to return there. It was a terrible kind of torment, like glimpsing paradise from the depths of a burning hell-hole.

His firm mouth twisted wryly, for he wasn't given to flights of fancy. Then, without turning his head, he asked, 'What do you want?'

Vargas jumped. Supposing Ben to be safely lost in

thought, he'd sidled close enough to assess what his customer amounted to in money.

His stock-taking had begun with the horses. They were big and sleek and so unlike the common mustangs descended from wild Spanish stock that they must have been specially bred. Valuable horses, with a valuable saddle embossed with dulled metal, which Vargas's experienced eye knew for silver.

The man's fine leather boots took his attention next, then the rifle in its scabbard and the heavy sheepskin coat strapped to the pack-horse. Vargas would have killed for any of these things if he'd had the courage, but his was ever the vulture's role, closing for the pickings when there was no resistance left. There were others enough to do the dangerous work in a land where life was cheap, possessions prized.

That the man had not been robbed already testified to how good he was at protecting himself, and once again Vargas silently berated himself for not hiding Sanna. The feeling was growing on him that this was the man he'd been told would be coming, although he was days earlier than expected.

Between his fear and his avarice, it was Vargas's own preoccupation that had caught him out and made him jump when he was spoken to. The question was ordinary enough and the voice which spoke it quiet, but it was the quietness of authority. Only a man accustomed to command and not request spoke like that.

If Vargas hadn't already been feeling inferior he would have done so now, and he forced his loose lips to roll back into an ingratiating smile. 'I came to ask, señor, why you stand in this murderous sun? My house is humble, for I am a poor man, but it is cool and a meal is being prepared for you.'

'I'll see my horses fed first.' Ben led them from the stream to a tethering rail under the shade of a lean-to at the side of the house. He took off his dust-coated poncho and flung it over the saddle, revealing a bandolier across his broad chest, each slot neatly filled with a bullet, and a revolver with its holster tied to his right thigh.

Vargas was noting these extra inducements to murder, when Ben's next words confirmed his suspicions. 'You have something for me. Fetch it.'

Displaying the palms of his hands disarmingly, Vargas hedged, 'What would I have for you, señor?'

'The name is Maddox.' Ben offered no further explanation, nor was it needed.

Vargas ceased blustering and hurried away, the rolls of fat on his body rising and falling like ripples on a disturbed pool. His sandalled feet sank deeply into the fine sand, and fresh sweat oozed from his overstimulated pores. He hated Americans. They could kill each other in as many vendettas as they wished, provided it was not on his doorstep.

Brave men, he believed, were fools. They did not die comfortably in bed after a full lifespan, as he fully expected to. His formula for survival was to offer resistance to nobody and to be useful to everybody. The violent men who came this way needed his supplies, and would need them again when they returned. Such needs kept him alive and flourishing.

His complacency was jolted when he entered the house and saw the shawl had slipped to Sanna's shoulders. As he passed on his way to the back room he pulled the shawl roughly over her gleaming hair and hissed, 'Remember what I told you. This man is very dangerous.

He will treat you like a whore if you encourage him. If that happens, I promise you will become one. You will no longer be good enough for my son and I shall sell you to every man who comes this way.'

Sanna, sublimely confident she wouldn't be here, ignored him. The American had seen her. That should be enough, but to be absolutely sure she was concentrating on her cooking. Her whole life had been attuned to regarding men as the lords of creation, entitled to homage from women in the form of obedience, hard work and good food.

Her contempt for Vargas had led her into a series of minor rebellions, but for the American she was not only willing to revert to the traditional role, she was worried in case she'd spiced the meat with too much chilli. On top of that, all her attention was needed to stop persistent flies from committing suicide in the bubbling beef.

Outside, Ben was also swatting away flies as he drew a bucket of water from the well. He held a handful to his mouth and tasted it warily. It was cool and fresh. He refilled his water-bottles and the stoppered goatskin he kept on his pack-horse. Water was shy in Mexico, hiding more often than showing itself. Ben knew where to look, but he took no chances. Hunger could be endured. Thirst killed.

He drank and washed his face. Sand found its way everywhere, gritting eyes, mouth, clothes and food. Sometimes he felt as though it were under his skin and he'd never be free of it.

Temporarily refreshed, Ben joined his horses in the shade to wait for Vargas, so that he could be sure they were properly fed. His care of them was as scrupulous as conditions allowed, for his life depended on their fitness.

Once more his mind strayed to his home far to the north in New Mexico. He wondered whether his father, Thomas, was still alive or whether his iron willpower had finally drained away with his physical strength.

Thomas had been a widower with four young children at home in Boston when, as an officer in the elite US Army Corps of Topographical Engineers, he had discovered the *estancia* while on a surveying and mapping expedition.

The aristocratic Spanish grandees who had lived there like princes for generations had all but died out, and there was only Luisa left to continue the proud line. She had fallen passionately in love with Thomas, who had married her. She wasn't beautiful, but he loved the land.

Ben was only five when, with his brothers and sister, he had been brought to New Mexico. He had swiftly put down his roots and could scarcely remember Boston or his real mother.

As for Thomas, he reigned supreme in his miniature kingdom while his children grew up assimilating a mixture of American and Spanish–Mexican culture, developing a goodly share of arrogance and pride from both.

The Maddox children appeared to be favoured by the gods. On the one hand they were hardy, as everybody reared on the edge of civilisation had to be; on the other they were pampered, as befitted their wealthy station in life. They were also a handsome brood, and secure, or they seemed to be until the turbulence of the Civil War had violently pruned the branches of the family tree.

Ben's reflections were halted by a slight sound. He spun round, then relaxed, for it was the girl peeping round the corner of the lean-to.

Sanna knew she was risking punishment, but with Vargas busy in the back room she had been unable to resist another look at her man. She was so very sure he was *hers* that she wasn't inhibited by any shyness as she smiled and said, 'Hello, I'm . . .'

She got no further, for there was a rush of footsteps. Vargas seized her arm and began pulling her back to the house. 'The food is spoiling,' he told her, using for Ben's benefit a light scolding tone that hid his anger.

'Mister!' Sanna began, but she was thrust back inside the house before she could finish her appeal.

Ben heard the sound of a scuffle, then there was silence. Vargas reappeared to apologise briefly, 'You know how it is with females, señor. They would rather be gossiping than working, and this one is a . . . a little foolish, you understand. I have hidden well the thing that was left for you, but it will take me only a few seconds more to retrieve it.'

Bowing, he backed away, partly reassured that Ben had not interfered, but fearing that Sanna had not ceased her trouble-making. A few blows about the body where they would not show had temporarily subdued her, but who could tell with such a rebellious female?

Ben had a little more difficulty in dismissing the girl from his mind this time, because it was so easy to picture Clare in her place. But she wasn't Clare, and that was the end of it. His sister was dead, and so were his two elder brothers. He was Thomas's heir now, and he had a certain duty to perform, a duty he couldn't allow to be complicated by the misfortunes of an unknown girl.

Ben, in his way, was as much an exile as Sanna, and violence had disrupted his life as much as hers. The difference between them was that where she had bowed with the suppleness of a young sapling before the blows of fate, he had met them head on so that all the finer qualities in him became stunted to enable the harsher ones to grow.

Sanna constantly expected the best to happen; Ben was always prepared for the worst. By the time their paths crossed in the dust-bowl squalor of Vargas's trading-store in the summer of 1867, Ben no longer had a finer side to his nature for her to appeal to.

He had abandoned dreams for reality, hope for certainty, honour for expediency and tenderness for toughness. His creed was survival, and the past six years had taught him that, whatever else was swept away, the land remained, and so it was only his own portion of that land that he cared for.

He was old and experienced far beyond his twenty-four years. He asked for no mercy and he gave none. He was also every bit as committed to ending his exile as Sanna was hers.

Ben was watching when Vargas approached this time, and the storekeeper realised that his eyes were that particular shade of blue which appeared to look through rather than at something. It was unnerving, like the eyes of the dead gazing into eternity and seeing something nobody else could.

Vargas wished he would stop having such thoughts and, like all superstitious people, sought to appease a force he felt was more powerful than himself. He sagged into one of his ready bows, and said earnestly, 'I wish you to accept, señor, that in this matter I am an unwilling go-between. I am not involved and have no desire to be.'

Ben merely held out his hand.

Vargas placed a ring in it as regretfully as though he

were parting with a pound of his own flesh, although he had already made plans for its return with no danger to himself. The ring would not be damaged, but Sanna—what if this Maddox demanded her also? For his son he was prepared to wait for the realisation of his tortured fantasies, but that another should enjoy her after all his vigilance! That would be harder to endure than his frustration.

Ben's hand closed round the ring. 'The message?'

'Señor Kirby will be waiting at the village of San Mari-Luz.'

'Where's that?'

Vargas turned and pointed. 'You follow the stream to the mountains. The village is somewhere among them, I am not sure where. You will have to ask again.'

'Anything else?'

Vargas shuddered once again as the eyes with the coldness of the dead and the clarity of the living settled on him. He licked his lips. 'You did not say you understood that I am not personally involved.'

'I understand. Get on with it.'

'I was told it would soon be the turn of another Maddox to beg.' Vargas flinched as he spoke, expecting a blow. When none came, he studied the American's face. It was impassive, and he was encouraged to disguise his own evil intent by offering advice he knew would not be taken. 'You have chased the coyote into his hole. Would it not be wise to leave him there and go home?'

Coyote, Ben thought, the wolf of the prairie. The fat man had an apt turn of phrase. He said, 'The only way to be sure a coyote stays in a hole is to bury him in it.'

'The grave could be yours.'

'Meanwhile,' Ben said pointedly, 'my horses are still hungry.'

Vargas fluttered his hands placatingly and hurried away.

Only when Ben was alone did his long fingers uncurl from the ring. It was Clare's. The final goad from Harry Kirby to keep him on the hunt—as if he needed goading.

Even in the shade, the splendid sapphire and its attendant diamonds burned like blue and white fire, searing the protective cover from memories he had buried deep in case the anger they aroused affected his caution.

Clare, his sister, younger than him by a year. Tall, fair-haired and lovely enough to attract Kirby, whose survival from his subsequent exploits had the touch of genius—or insanity.

Clare had been sixteen, and Kirby one of those foot-loose men who arrived from time to time at the *hacienda* looking for work and rarely staying long. Thomas Maddox kept his kingdom peaceful by allowing local Indians a yearly quota of cattle and full access to the water, and also by employing guards to patrol the huge valley.

Kirby had become one of those guards, and it hadn't crossed Thomas's mind that he was just the sort of man to cause a growing girl moments of speculation. Big, handsome, with brown eyes and curling black hair, he also had the advantage of being many years older than the few boys available for Clare to practise her coquettish arts on.

The tragedy was that she was too innocent to realise what manner of man she was meddling with, and when

Thomas had come upon Kirby kissing her, he had struck him down. Clare's screams had brought her three older brothers running.

Kirby had declared that they were going to be married, but Clare's denial had been proud and swift. Humiliated at being caught kissing an employee, she had stalked away. Thomas had had Kirby run off the property, laughing at his claims that he would be back for Clare and that he would make her whole family suffer for making a fool of him.

Kirby's ravings had been swiftly forgotten, for the year was 1861 and the Civil War started, splitting the States and the Maddox family.

Thomas joined his old regiment, expecting his eldest son, Gary, to fight with him in the Union army while the middle son, Joseph, stayed at home to run the ranch. Ben, barely seventeen, was dismissed as too young for war.

But Gary, having no strong northern ties like his father, had kissed his fiancée goodbye and slipped away to join the Confederacy to fight for the South. Ben, similarly-minded, had run off after him.

Gary and Ben had fought with the dashing but often threadbare Confederate cavalry while their father surveyed and mapped for the Union. Two years later Gary was killed. Ben wrote home, but made no further contact with his family, for New Mexico was held by Union troops throughout the war.

It wasn't, in fact, until several months after the war was over that Ben returned. The carefree boy, embittered by defeat and toughened by deprivation, rode back a veteran. He hadn't known whether he'd be welcomed as a prodigal or thrown out as a traitor.

Nevertheless, home called to him as powerfully as had once the drums of war.

But there had been no peace for him there. Instead, he'd learned what Harry Kirby had been up to while each of the Maddox men had followed what he'd seen to be his duty.

Kirby had joined the Confederates, but had been thrown into prison for rape and looting, escaping before his court-martial and fleeing to Mexico. There he'd remained until 1866, when he'd crossed the border again at the head of a band of *comancheros*, outlaws of all races whose only common bond was greed.

They raided the war-weakened southern territories in a grand sweep from Texas on the Gulf of Mexico in the east to California on the Pacific coast in the west. Kirby had made a special point of taking in the Blue Tree Valley in New Mexico. The *hacienda* itself, built like a fortress to withstand Indian attacks in its early days, had held out, but the Maddox family, returning from a visit to Santa Fé, had been caught in the open . . .

Ben looked again at the ring in his palm and his eyes were as hard and glittering as the sapphire. Vargas, approaching with two buckets of bran mixed with water, halted involuntarily. He sensed danger, though he couldn't think why, for Maddox appeared as calm and controlled as when he'd left him.

He watched the strong fingers close over the ring, met the eyes that were raised to his, and felt the compulsion to talk, to do or say anything that would avert what he felt was a very real, if unknown, danger.

As he placed a bucket before each horse, he searched his mind for something that would make this man feel he was on his side. Only one subject presented itself, and he said sympathetically, 'This Harry Kirby that you seek, señor, is a bad man, the very worst. He boasted much while he was here.'

He was given no encouragement to continue, but the compulsion was still so strong that he licked his lips and added, 'He said that he raided your home and killed your brother and stepmother and carried off your sister and . . . and . . .' Vargas's voice died away and he had to swallow before he could conclude, 'And left your father to die slowly of his wounds so that he would have plenty of time to understand what had happened to his family. This is true, señor?'

'My father didn't die.'

The words were softly spoken, but Vargas would have felt less menaced if they had been shouted. 'The Blessed Virgin be thanked for that,' he breathed piously, 'and also for your safety. Kirby believes you are the only one left. He says the destruction of your family is a matter of honour with him.'

'He wouldn't know what honour was,' Ben said dryly.

'True,' Vargas agreed, wishing he could feel he had made a friend, but knowing he hadn't. 'Your horses are feeding well. Is it not time you refreshed yourself with the meal that awaits you?'

'I'll be along.' But as Vargas bowed and retreated, Ben remained where he was, staring moodily at the mountains. Kirby was among them somewhere, waiting, unaware that his raid on the Maddox home had provided a bridge of reconciliation between Ben and his father.

Thomas, desperately weakened by his wounds and dogged by a persistent fever, had told Ben that the small army he had organised to go after Kirby and bring back

Clare had returned empty-handed. And this time there was no dissension over where Ben's duty lay. Thinking untrained men more of a hindrance than a help, he had set off alone to find his sister and punish Kirby.

He had no trouble following the *comancheros'* trail across Arizona, through Nevada and into California, for they raided any dwelling or village unable to stand against them. Sometimes other men joined him, but ultimately Ben was the only one who did not become discouraged and go home as one weary month followed another.

In California, the gang split up. Kirby stayed on with Clare and a few men, but when he discovered he was being pursued he went south into Mexico, safe from American law. The game of hide and seek continued until Kirby learned exactly who it was who was pursuing him so doggedly.

The temptation to torment another Maddox must have been irresistible, for he began leaving messages for Ben, each one accompanied by a trinket. In this way Ben recovered his brother Joseph's watch, his step-mother Luisa's necklace, brooch and earrings. He knew he was being drawn into a trap, and the message this time indicated it would soon be sprung.

Ben wondered whether Kirby had tired of his protracted revenge or whether the war of nerves had rebounded on himself. Yet, whatever was going on in that vicious and twisted mind, leaving Clare's ring for Ben was the equivalent of throwing down the gauntlet. One of them had to die so that the other could get on with his life.

Pocketing the sapphire, Ben slid his rifle from its

scabbard and walked towards the doorway of the house. He was planning an ending, while Sanna, eagerly awaiting him, was hoping for a beginning.

CHAPTER
THREE

BEN DUCKED through the doorway and paused while his eyes adjusted to the dimness after being narrowed against the brilliance of the sun. He straightened cautiously and found that his head just cleared the low ceiling.

The girl was sitting on the floor before the fire, and the face she turned towards him was flushed from cooking. Shrouded as she was in black, her eyes seemed unusually bright. Ben wondered at the excitement blazing in them until he noticed her lips were parted in a smile far too friendly for a modest girl. She must, he guessed, be as much for sale as the bottles on the shelves and was expecting to earn some money from him.

Vargas stood in the middle of the room trying to play the genial host to Ben and intimidate Sanna at the same time. It didn't work, for neither paid the slightest attention to him, not even when he bowed to Ben and indicated the long benches on either side of the table with a sweeping gesture of invitation.

Ben brushed past him to walk to the archway at the back of the room. He pulled the curtain aside and his nostrils were assailed by a stench almost as bad as the pig pen, except that here the reek of stale alcohol and vomit were paramount.

The room was cluttered with chests and boxes, and piles of clothes and trade blankets were stacked on every available surface. Lying on a rusted iron bed amid the clutter, her mouth wide open, her breathing slow and heavy, was an Indian woman who was as oblivious to Ben as she was to the flies crawling over her.

The scene was a surprise after the cleanliness of the girl and the other room and, suppressing his disgust, Ben picked his way carefully around obstacles until he reached another curtained archway. He eased the curtain aside and looked in. It was a storeroom, neat but smelling strongly of onions and all manner of dried foods. On the floor beneath a tiny shuttered window was a palliasse with a blanket neatly folded on top. This, presumably, was where the girl performed her other duties when her cooking was done.

Satisfied there was nobody here but the storekeeper, the girl and the unconscious woman, he returned to the main room. He sat on a bench by the wall where Sanna had set a place for him, putting his rifle across the table close to his right hand.

Vargas thumped his chest and protested with a fine display of ruffled dignity, 'I am José Vargas, a humble man but an honest one. You have nothing to fear here, Señor Maddox.'

He might have spared his breath, for Ben said only, 'I need supplies. Dried meat, beans, vestas, oats for the horses, and fruit if you've got it. Tomorrow won't do. I want them now.'

Such was always the way with Americans, Vargas thought contemptuously. No time for the little courtesies of life that were so essential to a Mexican. One could talk civilly to a man, even if one were planning to cut his throat. 'They will be fetched,' he promised, but he didn't move.

'I'm not stopping all day,' Ben told him pointedly.

Vargas darted a look at Sanna, who was busy transferring food from pans to plates. He was in a quandary. He didn't want to demean himself by taking over so domestic a chore; neither did he want to leave her with Maddox. He tried to delay, hoping Sanna would stop taking such an unconscionable time serving the food so that he could send her from the room.

'You would like cigars? Tequila?' He waved a hand at the shelves. 'There is also whisky from Texas.'

'Just what I ordered,' Ben answered flatly.

Smothering his annoyance and shifting his great bulk into motion, Vargas threw Sanna a warning look and disappeared reluctantly into the private quarters.

The curtain had scarcely settled behind him when Sanna sprang up and hurried over to Ben with all the high-spirited bounce of a puppy sure of an affectionate welcome. 'I thought he would never go!' she exclaimed. 'I thought you were never going to get here, either. I've been waiting just about for ever.'

Ben studied her suspiciously. 'I don't know you.'

'What's that got to say to anything? I know you. At least,' she added fairly, 'I *nearly* do, for you're exactly like the man I knew would be coming one day to take me home. I never gave up waiting and hoping, no matter what! It won't take me any time at all to pack. Anywhere over the border will be home for me, so I won't be too much bother. You will take me?'

The question was nothing more than an afterthought. In Sanna's mind the matter was already settled. Vargas's fumblings and the high price he had paid for her attested to her desirability, and as Ben was a young man she innocently assumed she would be twice as desirable to him.

Ben had been expecting a proposition, but not this one. His instinct for survival had already analysed and rejected her, even for half an hour with a rogue like Vargas hovering in the background. He ignored her excited little speech and said, 'The food.'

'Oh!' Sanna spun back to the fire and swooped on the plates. 'You men and your food,' she chatted. 'Well, I want you to eat your fill, but I'd be grateful if you'd be quick about it. I don't want to spend one second longer in this place than I have to.'

She thrust a dish of scrambled eggs seasoned with chilli in front of him and flanked it with a platter of tortillas, the flat maize pancakes she cooked to accompany every meal. As Ben began to eat, she made another trip to the hearth and returned with a generous portion of frijoles, mashed black beans, and tacos, which were more tortillas with a savoury meat filling.

She stood back smiling, anticipating his appreciation of the food, herself, and his promise to take her with him. Long seconds passed. He ate steadily, saying nothing. She glanced at the curtain and prompted anxiously, 'What do you say? I don't have much time. Vargas will beat me if he catches me talking to you.'

So she wasn't for hire, Ben thought, presumably because Vargas hadn't had her long enough to be willing to share her yet. It would come, if he'd read the avarice in the storekeeper's eyes correctly, but it was still no business of his. He wasn't here to put the world to rights, only his own portion of it. Reaching for the water jug, he advised, 'If talking gets you into trouble, don't talk.'

Sanna couldn't believe her ears. Snatching the jug ahead of him, she poured water into his glass, protesting, 'What kind of a man are you? You can see I don't belong here. I have to get back over the border.'

'I'm not going over the border.'

'Wherever you're going, then. Anywhere has to be better than here, and sooner or later you'll go home. Everybody does, and you're an American the same as me.'

'I hope you have more luck with the next fellow through,' Ben replied, pulling the tacos towards him and continuing to eat.

The colour faded from Sanna's cheeks. It had never occurred to her that she might be rejected. She clambered over the bench to sit opposite him, legs flashing white as she hoisted her skirt immodestly in her haste. She pushed the rifle aside and leaned across the table to him, shaking the shawl from her fair hair. 'Look at me. I'm one of your own people. You can't leave me here.'

'I didn't bring you.'

'I didn't want to come, so I don't see what that's got to do with it,' Sanna retorted, having precious little use for logic. In her desperation she grasped his shoulder and shook it. 'Vargas won't try to stop you. He's afraid of you. He's only brave with women, the miserable little bully. I hardly ever see anyone because usually he makes me hide when customers come. You must help me! You're my only chance.'

Ben removed her hand from his shoulder and deliberately put the rifle back in place as if he hadn't heard a word. She could have been Clare, he thought again, and would probably turn out just like her, savaging the hand that tried to help. He looked at her impassively, waiting for her to get discouraged and go away.

Sanna couldn't read his expression and, extraordinarily, it didn't seem to matter, for she was entranced by the cold blue eyes that Vargas feared so much. They seemed to be drawing the very soul from her. It was a peculiar feeling, causing her heart to flutter and her body to tingle, so that she could have gone on looking at him for ever. She was drowning in his eyes, and loving it.

She waited for him to show some sign that she was having a similar effect on him. When none came, she was puzzled. How could she be drawn so strongly to him without him being drawn to her? She was so uncomplicated herself and, lacking any understanding of the complexities of human nature, she assumed she must be doing something wrong and it was up to her to put it right.

She scrambled back over the bench, threw her shawl across the table and with hurried fingers undid her long braid so that her thick hair slid like a silk screen across her shoulders and down her back.

Sanna knew her hair was beautiful and its colouring rare. Lacking any charm to wear at her throat to bring her luck, she displayed her hair as if it were a talisman capable of working wonders. 'Look at me properly, Mr Maddox,' she pleaded, and repeating the name Vargas had used gave her the comforting feeling of appealing to a friend rather than a stranger.

Ben pushed away his empty plates and looked. She twisted and twirled before him with a strange mixture of provocation and anxiety, and if she hadn't represented a complication he couldn't afford, Ben would not have needed any further tempting. As it was, he refilled his glass with water and drank with the calm assurance that characterised him.

Sanna hovered between exasperation and panic, but she was in no position to give up. 'I'm strong and healthy,' she told him earnestly. 'I can cook and clean, sew, skin any kind of animal and cure meat. I wash myself every day, sometimes twice a day. What's more, you won't find a prettier woman anywhere, no matter how hard you look—and I promise, I truly promise, not to be a bit of trouble.'

Ben smiled slightly. 'You'll always be trouble. Women like you can't help it.'

She took the smile to mean he was softening, and wheedled, 'I'll take a pride in proving you wrong. Shall I get my things?'

'No. Pretty, clean or whatever, I don't travel with women.' His tone brooked no argument, and he watched the light go out of her. She seemed to crumple in on herself like a broken thing. He watched her warily, not sure whether she was going to cry or attack him.

Sanna did neither. Stubbornly convinced that he still didn't understand her predicament, she twisted round and lifted her foot so that he could see the sole. There was an old burn mark on it. She put it down and lifted the other, where there was a more recent one.

'See what happens when I run away? I get lost in that wilderness out there. Vargas finds me and burns me. If there was any way I could escape by myself I'd do it, but I can't. You must help me! I don't know what he'll do this time if he finds I've talked to you.'

'You're about to find out,' Ben said, his eyes on the curtain.

She followed his gaze and her blood ran cold. There was no mistaking the bulge that showed Vargas was behind it. She didn't know how much he had heard, but as he came into the room his heavy footsteps were like a knell of doom to all her hopes.

No more than Sanna did Vargas believe a man could actually reject her. Yet although he couldn't quite believe his luck, he felt uneasier than ever. Maddox had refused cigars, alcohol and now a beautiful girl. How could one deal with a man who showed no weaknesses, when weaknesses were what made up a human being?

Vargas, finding his thoughts once more veering towards the superstitious, retreated to an area where he felt safe. 'Fetch the coffee,' he ordered Sanna, knowing she had no choice now but to obey.

Sanna turned dejectedly to the fire, overwhelmed by shock that the man she had chosen did not want her. She wouldn't let herself believe it, because if she did there would be no hope for her. She would have to go on existing in this wretched hovel until the threat of Eduardo became a reality. She would be beaten into submission and her fine dreams would dry up like the desert and turn to dust.

She poured coffee from a smoke-blackened pot into a mug and carried it to Ben. Further along the table, Vargas was wrapping the supplies. Anything was preferable to the son of such a man, but as she looked again at Ben she knew if she had a hundred men to pick from, he would still be her choice. Some quality in him reached out and touched and held her. Suddenly she couldn't bear to lose him—she really couldn't. At the thought of it, her fear of being left to Vargas's vengeance was overlaid by an indescribable sadness.

It goaded her to one last act of defiance. She seized Ben's arm and burst out, 'I don't think I could have explained properly. If you take me with you I'll do anything, anything at all. You won't have to chase me around as he'—her thumb jerked disparagingly at Vargas—'tries to. I won't scream or fight or cause you any fuss. We'll be fine together. Please!' Her voice broke on the last word.

Ben removed her hand from his arm and wished she'd stop making things worse for herself. She must be as stupid as she was lovely. He saw the purple of suppressed anger mottle Vargas's complexion and wasn't surprised when he growled, 'See to the dishes, girl, and stop making a pest of yourself.'

For a moment Sanna's eyes remained on Ben's. Then, slowly, as if defeat were too heavy a burden to bear, she began to stack the dishes and trailed out of the room to wash them in the stream.

Vargas shook his head as he watched her go, and told Ben, 'You are right to have nothing to do with that girl. In my humanity I rescued her from the Indians, and at a price a poor man like myself could not afford. I have housed and fed and protected her, and work her only lightly, but is she grateful? No! Her angel face hides the soul of a devil, for she is nothing but trouble. I am like a father to her, and what must she do but shame me before one such as yourself. I do not know what lies she has been telling you . . .'

'It's none of my business,' Ben broke in coldly. He drank his coffee, put some coins on the table and picked up his rifle. 'Get those supplies on my pack-horse.'

'Certainly, certainly.' Vargas was piqued at having his eloquence stemmed in full flood. On the other hand he was eager to be rid of Maddox. Then he would only have to wait for his wife to recover for Sanna to be punished as she deserved. His wife would help willingly when she learned what the girl had been up to.

She would also choose the punishment. Since she was anxious for Eduardo's home-coming gift to bear no obvious disfigurement, no doubt it would be the hot poker on the foot again. The thrill in it for Vargas was that Sanna always took a good deal of restraining, and he was able to handle her freely under his wife's eyes.

Agreeable mental pictures spurred his legs, over-burdened though they were with so much weight, into something close to a run as he rounded the house to the lean-to. His anticipation of his coming pleasure did not prevent him frowning over another task that had to be done, and quickly.

Sanna was at the stream, washing plates and spreading them to dry on the sand. As Ben came out of the house he saw her looking at him, but ignored her. He didn't want to set her off again. She had gone through so many emotions in such a short space of time that there could only be bitterness left.

He was wrong. Bewilderment, not accusation, filled Sanna's eyes. Her development from child to woman had taken place far from the vicinity of any attractive man. Ben was the first to awaken a positive response in her, with all the heady promise that entailed. His reward for this feat was to have heaped on his unsuspecting head all the god-like qualities Sanna had generously bestowed on the dream figure of her rescuer.

She saw him as the physical embodiment of the fantasy hero who had made her existence bearable by being her constant companion. His refusal to assume this role did not flaw him in her eyes, for she could accept no fault in her hero, and so she wondered what was wrong with herself.

She touched her cheek. Had she been careless enough to let the sun darken and freckle her skin? She didn't think so, and her fingers felt as soft as her cheek. She smothered her hands in animal grease at night to counter the roughness caused by the manual work she did.

Perplexed, she came to the conclusion that although she could ignore the stubble on his face and the dust on his clothes and visualise him as a gentleman, he took her at face value and was unable to see her as a lady.

She jumped up and called, 'Mr Maddox!'

Vargas heard her and looked round the side of the house. He saw Ben pause and half swing towards her. He drew back, seizing his chance to draw a small mirror from inside his shirt and flash a quick message to the mountains. He was petrified he would be caught, but the sound of Sanna speaking again reassured him.

'Mr Maddox, would it have made any difference if my dress had been silk?'

'No,' Ben said shortly, and it was true. Sanna was desirable enough in her too-tight blouse and too-short skirt. She didn't need wrapping up in silk.

'What if my hair had been curly?' she persisted. 'I can curl it, you know, with rags . . .'

He shook his head and walked on.

Sanna's slender hands curled into fists as she exclaimed, 'Didn't anybody ever tell you never to look a gift horse in the mouth?'

Stung, Ben retorted, 'It's the mouth that bothers me. It talks too much.'

Instantly her manner changed, a coaxing smile replacing her belligerent expression. 'I can be quiet,' she promised with less than her usual truthfulness. 'I can go hours at a time without saying a word.'

Ben cursed himself for getting involved in a pointless argument, and finished it by reiterating flatly, 'I don't travel with women.'

He reached the lean-to where Vargas was tut-tutting as he tied the supplies on the pack-horse. 'I'm sorry the girl still pesters you, señor,' he began. 'You can see what a trial she is to me.'

'I'll be back this way,' Ben replied evenly. 'I don't want to see any more burns on her feet.' It was a gesture, nothing more, for there was a swifter way home when his task was completed. Still, it might help her, and it didn't cost him anything.

The pouches above and below Vargas's eyes widened until yellow showed around his black pupils as he protested, 'You do not believe I would do such a thing? No, no! It is my wife who punishes the girl, but only for her own good. Think of the dreadful things that could happen to her if she strays too far.'

'Whoever or whatever, no more burns,' Ben repeated, climbing into his saddle and taking the leading rein of the pack-horse from Vargas.

'Certainly no more. I have already told my wife so.'

Ben turned his horses and rode round the enclosures towards the mountains. Vargas remained under the shade of the lean-to, a genuine smile on his face as he watched him go. Occasionally he darted speculative glances at Sanna, until she left the stream and disappeared into the house.

Singing to himself, he hitched up his baggy cotton trousers and waddled after her. He didn't have to hurry

any more. He had all the time in the world, and savour-
ing what would happen to the girl when his wife awoke
was almost as good as experiencing it.

Sanna, stacking the pans by the fireplace, heard him
coming, but her blood could run no colder. She had
gambled for happiness and lost. Her special man had
gone. She was left with the horror of Vargas.

CHAPTER
FOUR

THE REEDY singing that warned Sanna of Vargas's
approach stopped before he reached the door. He
cleared his throat noisily and spat. She grimaced, and all
the loathing she felt for him surged anew, cutting
through the apathy she had sunk into.

She sprang to her feet, telling herself she was mad to
be sitting waiting to be swatted like a heat-dazed fly. Yet
what could she do? Something, anything! She ran to the
door and drove home the bolts. Next she seized the
sturdy plank propped against the wall and slotted it into
supports on either side of the door. It would take a
battering-ram wielded by more than one man to force an
entry now.

The two windows were too small for Vargas to
get through, and yet she felt safer when she had bolted
the shutters and reinforced them in the same way.
She heard Vargas try to open the door and then
thump on it in a manner that was more perplexed than
angry.

Sanna ran to the back of the house to secure the
window in the storeroom, which also doubled as her
bedroom. When it was done, she stood quivering with
reaction. She was part triumphant and part petrified.
She had gained herself a respite from punishment, but if

Vargas was unable to get in, she was equally unable to get out.

A bellow of rage and a thunderous pounding on the door told her that he had realised the house was barricaded against him. Not sure what to do next, Sanna left the storeroom. She was picking her way through the shambles of the main bedroom when a groan came from the bed. The noise Vargas was making had penetrated his wife's befuddled brain and her head was rolling from side to side as she came slowly out of her stupor.

Sanna forced herself to go over to the bed. She had seen the woman like this several times, but her revulsion never lessened. An empty bottle rolled away from her feet. Another, half-full, was on a chest beside the bed. She had to master the retching that threatened to convulse her as she reached for the bottle, for the pillow and Señora Vargas's blouse were encrusted with dried vomit.

With the bottle in one hand, Sanna was nerving herself to grasp the woman's foul hair to raise her head, when the eyes in the bloated face opened. They stared unseeingly at her, and the mouth gaped. Swiftly, Sanna tipped the bottle so that the whisky ran into the mouth. Some ran out, but Señora Vargas began to swallow. Sanna kept pouring until Señora Vargas's eyes closed, then she dropped the bottle on the bed and fled back to the main room, her own nausea threatening to overcome her. She hadn't actually touched the woman, but she felt contaminated.

She closed her ears to the abuse Vargas was hurling at her from outside and poured water into a bowl. She washed her face and hands and as she brushed and plaited her hair she began to feel better.

Her head turned in alarm as something heavier than Vargas's fists crashed against the door. It was followed by a howl of pain, and she guessed he was using his own tremendous weight to force an entry. He threw himself against the door again, and howled again, but though the stout timbers shuddered, they held.

Sanna sat on a bench. For the moment she could think of nothing else to do and her limbs began to tremble uncontrollably, as though her nervous system were seeking a release from unbearable tension. She hugged herself, waiting for the acceptance of her predicament to come and, with it, a kind of peace. She knew so much better than Vargas, who was still bruising himself against the door, the futility of exhausting a small strength against a greater one.

She was trapped. Her dreams of escape had been just that—dreams. It was pointless working herself into a state of hysteria as Vargas was doing. Sanna tried not to think of the bleakness of her future, tried not to speculate whether ultimately she would seek the bottle of oblivion like that ghastly creature in the next room.

She rebelled against the picture this conjured up in her mind, and thought once more of the man who was riding further and further away from her. Mr Maddox. Her man. She knew it. Why didn't he?

Sanna, accustomed as she was to bending before the blows of fate, was none the less single-minded. The fierceness of her feelings for the man who had rejected her kept at bay the resignation for which she was waiting. She simply couldn't accept the hopelessness of her plight.

Stubbornness firmed the softness of her youthful features, and her little chin set resolutely. She wouldn't tamely take her punishment while she waited for another chance. She didn't want another chance, she wanted this one—which had so inexplicably slipped away from her.

Bullied all her life rather than guided, at the best of times Sanna was little more than a bundle of instincts and impulses, yet she was capable of reducing a complex situation to manageable proportions by sorting out what she wanted most.

And, sitting shivering on the bench while Vargas hurled himself and his oaths at the door, she had very little sorting out to do, for the answer was crystal clear. She wanted Mr Maddox. To get him, she would have to go after him. To stay with him, she would have to refuse to be rejected. She would have to tag along until he came to his senses and realised, as she did, that they belonged together.

Sanna was dazzled by the simplicity of the solution. Her buoyant nature reasserted itself, driving out despair and bringing the brightness of hope back to her eyes. She stopped trembling and looked suspiciously at the door as Vargas abruptly ceased his assault upon it.

The silence after so much noise held a threat of its own but, short of burning down the trading-store with herself and his wife and all his possessions inside, she couldn't see how he could get at her. Ever an optimist, she didn't dissipate her new-found strength by worrying over what he might or might not be plotting next.

She had too much plotting of her own to do. One way or another, she had to trick him and get out of here. She would pack first, so that when an idea came she would be ready.

Rumbling snores came from Señora Vargas as Sanna

made her way to the storeroom, stopping briefly to lift items from the piles of trade goods that cluttered the room. A new blanket to replace her threadbare one, a black poncho with broad white stripes, a leather belt and a sheath knife, and a box of vestas.

There were many other things she could have taken, but she dared not load herself down too much. She would need all her speed and agility to outmanoeuvre Vargas.

Sanna didn't feel as if she were stealing. She had worked hard during her two years here, cooking and cleaning, hoeing and planting, tending livestock. She had been fed well, but she had been so skinny when she'd arrived that she suspected the ample food was to put some flesh on her before Eduardo returned. She had certainly grown taller and stronger and shapelier, yet she didn't feel beholden for that because her workload had been correspondingly increased.

She had never been treated as anything other than a slave, and she felt she was owed more than the few spoils she put on her mattress in the storeroom. She spread out her shawl and, in the middle, placed her only other blouse and a length of white cotton Señora Vargas had given her to sew into a dress for Eduardo's return. Much as she wanted pretty clothes, Sanna had found countless excuses for delaying the task, for she'd had no intention of making herself desirable for Eduardo.

She gathered the rest of her worldly possessions—hairbrush and toothbrush, a black felt hat with a wide floppy brim, a piece of black lace and a small pouch containing things she treasured from her turbulent past. Putting the hat aside, she tied the ends of the shawl together, making as small a bundle as she could.

She used string to tie the poncho and blanket into another bundle, leaving long ends dangling so that it could be secured to a saddle. The sheath of the knife slotted through the new belt, which sagged around her narrow waist when she tried to buckle it. She would have to make another hole.

Glancing round to make sure she had missed nothing, Sanna carried her things to the main room and put them on the table. Excitement was flickering through her again. Her eyes were sparkling and her cheeks flushed. She felt as if she were almost on her way.

Not a sound came from Vargas as she busied herself making another hole in the belt. It clasped her waist snugly when she tried it on again. Food was her next concern, and she juggled in her mind the importance of several days' supplies against the need to travel light.

Sanna took a corn loaf she had baked that morning and wrapped it with strips of dried meat, sunflower seeds and dried pumpkin.

She added as much pemmican—the nourishing cakes of dried and pounded meat she made for travellers by mixing it with melted fat and dried fruit—as she felt she could comfortably carry. She tied up the food and put it with the other bundles, frowning at how the pile of even barest essentials was growing.

She filled a gourd with water, pressed the stopper home and placed it on the table. That was it. She could carry no more if she couldn't dupe Vargas and had to make a run for it.

As she sat down to consider her next move, Vargas's silence was explained by the fact that he had been considering his. Violence and abuse had got him no-where, so after deep thought he switched to persuasion.

'Sanna, my little dove,' he cooed as though he were a dove himself. 'Let me in. You have nothing to fear. My temper has gone and it will not come back. I swear this on the honour of my mother and my mother's mother. What greater oath can a man make? None, my precious one. It is time for us to be reasonable, to forgive each other for this misunderstanding. Come now, let me in and we shall speak no more of this. What do you say?'

Sanna ignored him, his sugary words and dulcet tone scarcely penetrating her mind, which was pursuing ways and means of catching up with Ben. It was about noon. If he'd wanted to rest during the sizzling hours of the afternoon, surely he would have stayed here? She had seen the direction he had taken and, whatever he did, his horses were fine ones. He would be well into the foothills of the mountains long before nightfall.

He would be easy to follow if he stuck to the stream, but she was afraid she would never find him if he left it. She was no tracker. Worse, her previous escapes had come to nothing because, although she had been born with many gifts, a sense of direction was not among them.

She must catch up with him before he left the stream, and that was that. Surely she could depend on something to go right for her today! Satisfied that she wasn't asking too much of the gods when she was risking everything herself, she mentally reviewed the three horses in the corral.

One was a mare, very old and slow. Vargas had ridden her out early this morning, presumably to get away from his wife's ravings before she mercifully passed out. One good thing about that was that Vargas was lazy. He would have left his saddle and bridle over the corral fence for Sanna to put away. They would be handy when she made her dash for freedom.

The second horse was still slightly lame from a stone Sanna had prised out from under one of its hoofs. This left a small but wiry mustang she called Magpie, because of his showy black-and-white colouring. Magpie it would have to be, then.

'Sanna,' Vargas began again, 'I understand how you are feeling. You liked Maddox, and that is natural enough, but only because you do not know Eduardo. Now there is a proper man! Once you have seen him you will forget the American. Good times are coming for you. I beg you not to spoil them by continuing this naughtiness.'

How long, Sanna thought, would it take to saddle up Magpie? Too long if she had Vargas after her. Perhaps he would be unable to stay awake during the long hot hours of the afternoon, though, for his mind and body were conditioned to expect a siesta. Hunger might keep him wakeful for he was as greedy as he was lazy. If she could get some food out to him, habit should ensure that he slept.

She wrapped more food into a cloth and stood listening for a few moments to what Vargas was saying, trying to judge his mood. His voice was full of entreaty, and loaded with a sympathy utterly alien to his character, as he called, 'Sanna, you must not be sad for Maddox. He did not want you. A beautiful girl should never have to beg. Eduardo will treat you like a princess, worship at your feet. Do you hear me, daughter of my heart? A little more patience, and my son will give you everything you desire. He will be your slave, your most willing slave.'

Sanna crept towards one of the shuttered windows.
Vargas, getting no response to his fulsome promises, lost
the patience he was counselling her to employ. His fist
crashed on the door and his voice rose to a shriek of
rage. 'You want to sulk for the American—then sulk.
No, grieve, for soon he will be dead! Manolito and
Miguel are waiting in the mountains to rob and kill him.
Do you hear me—kill! I have arranged it. You pine for a
dead man, you stupid bitch!'

Sanna nearly dropped the piece of wood she had lifted
from the slots at the window as she froze at his words. He
might simply be seeking to weaken her resolve, and yet
there had for the first time been the ring of truth in his
voice. Manolito and Miguel were relatives of Señora
Vargas, deadly Apaches who often hung about the
trading-store.

It was they who had told Vargas about Sanna and
arranged her sale. If they were planning to ambush Mr
Maddox, then her need to escape became all the more
urgent—for his sake as well as hers.

Allowing time for her quivering nerves to settle, she
eased the wood down and steeled herself for what she
must do: unbolt the shutters, throw out the food, bolt
the shutters again, and all in the second or two it would
take Vargas to get from the door to the window.

If he could keep the shutters open he could spy on her
and taunt her, perhaps throw things at her. It was in his
nature to torment her, and this precious feeling of safety
she had would be gone.

For the moment he was being very quiet, just when
she needed him to be noisy to cover the sound of what
she was doing. Holding her breath, she began to ease
back the bolk. It grated slightly. She stopped, listening,

then fetched some grease to smear on the bolt. Cautiously she tried again, and it moved noiselessly.

Sanna wiped her hands on the bundle of food, anxiety filming her face with perspiration. Swiftly she opened the shutters, the bundle poised to fling outside. She screamed with shock and pain as Vargas's hand grabbed her hair and jerked her cruelly towards him.

The bundle dropped outside as she tried to stop herself being dragged through the window with one hand while the other sought wildly for the knife at her waist. Vargas was crowing with triumph as she found it. She lashed awkwardly at him and the knife sank into his fleshy upper arm.

He screamed and let her go. Sanna wiggled back inside, slamming, bolting and barring the shutters. She sank into a ball on the floor, hugging herself and whimpering with fear. It took her long moments to realise that she was safe, and her fingers trembled uncontrollably as she tried to massage her painful scalp.

The sound of Vargas sobbing outside did a lot to calm her. Soon he would realise that the wound was not serious. The knife had not touched bone. The fat she despised had protected him. When he had stopped the bleeding and bound up his arm, he would probably eat to comfort himself. Then, if he stayed true to form, he would be unable to stop himself from sleeping.

Sanna stood up jerkily, her nerves still recovering from the pain and terror of being almost dragged through the window. She had so nearly been at Vargas's mercy, and she shuddered anew to think what would have happened to her then. She sat on a bench, leaning over the table and hugging her bundles to her as if they were a passport to safety.

Vargas's sobs softened to moans, then ceased altogether. Presumably he had discovered that he was not dying. Sanna forced herself to wait patiently, and this was the hardest part, for it seemed as though her very spirit was yearning to flee to Mr Maddox. She didn't think beyond finding him. For the moment, being with him meant more than her silk cushion, her white house, her fine dresses and all the other good things she was sure were coming to her.

An hour passed. The inside of the house was becoming like an oven. Outside it would be so much worse. Vargas could tolerate heat much better than he could tolerate pain, but even he must have sought shelter by now. The lean-to at the side of the house was the ideal place.

She went to the wall that supported the lean-to and listened. Eventually she was rewarded by the sound of heavy snores. It was now or never. She had planned to escape through one of the windows in this room, but memories of the recent tussle made her too frightened even to approach them.

What if he was trying to trick her again? She didn't think she could cope with another encounter like the last one, and she would be in even more danger if she risked opening the door. That left her with the window in the storeroom, which was very small, but she would have to take her chances. If Vargas was fooling her, he couldn't watch both sides of the house at once, and he probably thought she couldn't get through the back window.

She picked up her baggage and crept through the main bedroom. Señora Vargas was mumbling and her head was rolling on the pillow, though she was still far from consciousness. Sanna went on to the storeroom and eyed the window doubtfully. It was very small.

She would have a better chance of getting through if she stripped and greased her body, but dread of Vargas catching her naked made her clutch her clothes more tightly around her. It was one risk she simply couldn't take.

The storeroom was the closest she had ever come to having a place of her own, and she kept everything here in good order. The bolt on the shutter didn't squeak as she drew it back. She felt deafened by the painful thudding of her heart as she opened the shutters and looked out, swiftly glancing both ways.

Nothing. No Vargas lurking to trap her. She leaned out to drop her bundles one by one, grateful that the sand received them softly. Herself next. She held her knife in her hand as she put her head and arms through the window just in case Vargas surprised her. The thought of being caught stuck and helpless made her wriggle frantically, and she scarcely felt the pain as she forced her shoulders through the window.

She braced herself for another struggle with her hips, but she came free before she expected it and tumbled headlong on to her belongings, somersaulting on her back and coming to her feet gasping for breath. She crouched like a hunted animal, poised for flight, but everything was utterly still, and all that disturbed the silence was Vargas's snores.

Sanna's heart still thumped, but she felt so much better now she was in the open. She gathered her bundles and crept towards the lean-to, which she had to pass in order to reach the corral. She peered round the corner. There was no trickery in Vargas's snores. He was fast asleep.

As she forced herself to walk on stealthily, the hot sand reminded her of one thing she had forgotten. Her sandals. Not for the world would she go back for them, however. She had never been able to take as much care of her feet as she had of her hands and complexion, and the soles were tough enough to tolerate the heat. She could walk over rough stones without flinching.

As she passed the pig pen, Sanna glanced back and saw that Vargas hadn't moved. Feeling safer, she hurried on to the corral, where all the animals were clustered under a shelter of woven twigs and branches supported by stout poles.

Sanna dropped her bundles inside the corral and slipped through the rails next to the saddle and bridle Vargas had slung on the top bar. She took the bridle, left her baggage and, crooning softly, approached the animals.

Magpie made up for the ugliness of his large head, short-backed body and stocky legs with stamina and a sweet disposition. She didn't have to chase him. He nuzzled her as she put on the bridle. Elation bubbled within her as she led him towards the saddle and her bundles.

She was throwing Vargas's horse blanket over Magpie's back when suddenly one of the donkeys brayed, a harsh discordant sound that shattered the silence and disturbed the other dozing animals. Birds rose screeching from the roof of the shelter and the donkey brayed again, exciting another to join in.

Only Magpie seemed undisturbed by the commotion. Sanna heard Vargas shout. She flung the saddle over the horse and groped under his belly for the cinch, which she pulled towards her and buckled with frantic fingers.

Vargas was coming towards her at a run. It was an awesome sight, his flesh bouncing like a disturbed jelly as each foot hit the ground so heavily that every ounce of his massive body was jarred. He seemed to be carried along by his own momentum and he grabbed the rails of the corral to stop himself, his body crashing sideways into the fence.

With a sob of terror, Sanna grabbed her bundles and flung herself into the saddle. She saw Vargas trying to slip through the rails, but he was too fat, and he abandoned his attempt to climb over the top to run to the gate.

Sanna waited until he began to open it, then drove Magpie straight at the clustered animals, stampeding them towards the gate. One of her precious bundles slipped from her grasp, but she didn't notice it. Vargas was forced to leap back as the animals charged through the gate, herself with them.

She was away. Free! She laughed wildly, and the release from tension was so great that tears of happiness ran down her cheeks. She glanced back and laughed more sanely as she saw Vargas, a murky figure in the settling dust, shaking his fist at her. It would take him hours to round up his scattered stock, and he would have to do it himself. There would be no slave to toil for him.

She swerved Magpie towards the stream, and that was her undoing. In her haste she hadn't tightened the cinch sufficiently. The saddle slipped sideways and she was pitched on to the sand.

The impact winded her but she was on her feet in a trice, her elation turning once more to terror as she saw Vargas running towards her, whooping with glee. She swooped on her bundles, noticing that one was missing, but it had little importance for the moment. She chased after Magpie, who had come to a halt with the saddle hanging awkwardly to one side.

She would have blessed his placid temperament had she not been uttering more fervent prayers for deliverance from the fast-approaching Vargas. She had to drop her belongings once more to use all her strength to heave the saddle back in position, sweat making her fingers slip on the buckle as she tightened the cinch.

She could see that blanket under the saddle was caught up, but she had no time to correct it. She grabbed her bundles and launched herself on to the horse. Vargas was almost upon her. She kicked her heels into Magpie's sides and the animal sprang forward just as Vargas threw himself at his tail. As if by intent, the tail switched sideways, and the sand quivered as Vargas sprawled full length.

It was comic, but Sanna didn't laugh this time. It had been all too close, and she had had one scare too many. She rode on along the stream, not checking Magpie's pace until she at last felt safe.

She stopped and saddled him up properly, feeling weak with reaction. A wash in the stream soothed her. She tied her bundles securely to the saddle, then walked the horse for a while in penance for galloping him so furiously in such heat.

When she climbed into the saddle again and looked back, she could barely distinguish the hump of the trading-store. It was her last look back. She was beyond Vargas's reach at last. He had no horse that could catch Magpie.

She took stock of her situation, and it wasn't as good as it might have been. The missing bundle had contained her food. Mr Maddox was a good two hours ahead of her, and the rising foothills restricted her line of vision.

And, somewhere, Manolito and Miguel were lying in ambush while Ben knew nothing about them. The worry allowed her no respite to enjoy her freedom or gloat over how, for once, she had out-matched Vargas's cunning.

No, worry remained her constant companion as the sun passed its zenith and a slight breeze cooled her heated body. It was a curious feeling to be anxious about someone other than herself. The fretting and tension she endured as the hours passed would have convinced her, if she hadn't already been so sure, that she and Mr Maddox belonged together.

CHAPTER
FIVE

DISQUIET RODE with Ben, an unwanted but unshakeable companion. It prompted him to leave the well-defined trail as soon as the trading-store receded to no more than a vague hump in the distance, and skirt round the foothills, keeping roughly parallel with the stream but out of sight of it.

It was a time-wasting tactic dictated by his sense of survival and, although the afternoon wore peacefully on, he was irritated by the way the disquiet persisted. He considered whether it had anything to do with the girl, a latent twinge of conscience, perhaps, inspired by her superficial resemblance to Clare.

It would have been difficult enough to re-establish Clare among her own kind after what had happened to her, but for the girl it would be impossible. She had lived with the Indians before joining Vargas's *ménage à trois* and, if she succeeded in getting back over the border, respectable women would shun her.

She was, whether she knew it or not, more than an exile. She was an outcast. Vargas might have punished her defiance by burning her feet, but he might just as well have branded her forehead with a lifelong mark of shame.

She might look angelic, but she was a fallen angel, and

her own helplessness would be no defence against the scorn of decent women. Suicide was held to be the only way out for such a girl, and if she tried to insinuate her contaminating presence among them they would turn on her with self-righteous wrath.

But Ben was not a woman, and he knew he might have reacted differently to her had he been on his way home, his duty done. She was certainly lovely enough to beguile any man whose mind wasn't obsessed with revenge and family honour.

He stirred uneasily in the saddle as he allowed himself to contemplate what a delectable diversion she would be, a temptress amply endowed with all the necessary charms to assuage the lust burning inside a man too long on his own.

She had been shameless about putting herself on offer and she would find many takers, even if he wasn't among them. He suppressed a sigh along with the desire she aroused in him, for he had no intention of returning by way of the store.

There was a quicker way back and, in any case, dumping the girl before he got home might have proved difficult—and he would have had to get rid of her. Setting all other considerations aside, Linda was waiting for him.

A shutter in his mind closed on the image of the fair-haired girl with beseeching blue eyes and opened on a very different one . . . Linda with her elegantly coiled black hair, brooding brown eyes and creamy magnolia skin. She was twenty-two now, a poised and dignified woman, his childhood sweetheart fully grown up.

He hadn't asked her to wait for him, but she wanted so much to be mistress of Blue Tree Valley that she was

gambling more of her fast-vanishing youth on his returning alive—and willing to marry her. She had been frustrated too long and too often to abandon her last chance
of getting what she wanted.

Linda was a neighbouring rancher's daughter, and the
closeness of their ages, for he was just two years older,
had ensured that they'd more or less grown up together.
He had thought in a vague and youthful way that they
would one day marry, and it had been a shock when
she'd become engaged to his eldest brother, Gary. She
had been only fifteen then, but she was of Spanish–
Mexican blood and had matured early.

Ben had hidden his hurt, the feeling of rejection he
had been too inexperienced to cope with, believing that
Linda had been swept off her feet by the dashing and
happy-go-lucky Gary. It had been easy enough to understand, for he himself had been going through the stage of
hero-worship for his eldest brother.

His cynicism towards women, begun by his stepmother, had not been deepened by Linda until some
time later, when it dawned on him that Gary's superior
attraction stemmed from the fact that he was heir to the
hacienda and its lands.

Ben might never have known, had the wedding planned for when she was sixteen not been postponed by the
outbreak of the Civil War, when Gary had skipped off to
join the Confederates.

That year of 1861 had been as traumatic to Linda's
family as for his own, although in a different way. Her
father, the aristocratic Don Philip de Montoya, was a
weak and unworthy inheritor of a ranch pioneered by
his Spanish ancestors. He had drunk and gambled
away his lands and gone south into Mexico to recoup

the family fortunes, taking the reluctant Linda with him.

She had depended on her marriage to Gary to restore her to a position of pride and prestige, knowing that, furious as Thomas Maddox was with his favourite eldest son for joining what he considered the wrong side, he would not disinherit him. Gary's death had dashed her hopes, but after the war Don Philip had returned to New Mexico to set up a haulage business in Santa Fé. With the ever-increasing flow of settlers to the west, profits were good, and Linda was once more in a position to pursue her own ambitions.

In 1866 she visited the *hacienda* in Blue Tree Valley and became engaged to Joseph, the middle son and the heir. She had returned to Santa Fé to prepare her bride clothes when Harry Kirby and his *comancheros* struck, and she once more lost her fiancé.

She was at the *hacienda*, comforting the sick and shattered Thomas Maddox, when Ben finally rode home from the war. The unreality of the short time they spent alone returned to Ben with the vividness of a scene suspended for ever in time by its sheer unexpectedness.

He could hear again the tinkle of the water playing in the fountain, smell the flowers and see the simple beauty of the white-plastered colonial arches which shaded the rooms opening on to the elaborate patio where they walked, one of the many decorative patios enclosed by the sprawling *hacienda*.

Most of all he could see Linda, smell her musky perfume, feel the tantalising ripeness of her silk-clad body when she accidentally brushed against him. As a child she had been proud and autocratic, although no more so than himself, and with the years she had de-

veloped a dignity which made her rather remote and
untouchable.

Ben, intrigued against his will, suffered all that much
more of a shock when with precious little preamble she
had calmly proposed to him.

'You are the last of your line, Ben,' she said. 'It is your
duty to marry and provide sons for all this.' With a
graceful gesture she paused to indicate the grandness of
the *hacienda*, then continued, 'It is also your duty to
choose a wife who would be a fitting mistress for such a
home, one who has been trained since birth for such a
task. Myself, Ben. Many things have happened which
we couldn't have foreseen, but they have only served to
convince me it was always our destiny to marry.'

Ben, disillusioned after weary years of a war which
had turned out anything but the lark he'd imagined,
returning home at last to find anything but peace and
safety, should have been beyond shock—and yet he
found himself looking at Linda as though he'd never
seen her before.

For a few seconds he said nothing, for it took him that
long to recover from the revelation that she hadn't
chosen Gary for love, or Joseph for comfort, but that she
had cold-bloodedly selected a suitable home for herself.
Naturally he was next on the list.

A younger Ben would have reacted with hot anger, for
he had been close to his brothers, and they deserved
better than that, but he merely asked cynically, 'Don't
you think it's time to get a horse out of another stable?
You seem to be a jinx on anything bearing the Maddox
brand.'

'You're being fanciful,' she reproved him coolly. 'You
must think of the future, as I am, and consider what is

best for everybody. It is only my conviction that we were destined to marry which has given me the courage to speak so frankly. We're not children any more, Ben, and we've both learned that life isn't a game which will work out right without any effort on our part. Together we can overcome all of the losses of the past.'

'I'm not done with the past yet. You talk of duty— mine is to settle with Harry Kirby and get Clare back.'

'I understand that,' she began.

'Then you'll also understand that I'm no better bet than Gary or Joseph. I'd have thought another Maddox fiancé would be the last thing you'd want.'

The jibe missed the mark, for her dark eyes did not flinch from his. 'Allow me to be the best judge of what I want,' she replied, and he could only applaud her unshakeable poise. 'And also allow me to remind you how close we were as children.'

'You were just saying we're not children any more,' he reminded her, but he was merely quibbling, and he knew it. They were, as she had so precisely and practically pointed out, a suitable pair. A cold-blooded woman for a cold-blooded man, neither under any illusions about their possible marriage. She would be the perfect mistress of the *hacienda* and a dutiful mother to his sons, and he wouldn't have to pretend any emotions he did not feel.

His rational mind accepted that he couldn't make a better choice, and yet he shied away from committing himself. Too much was still in balance. 'I'll be gone a long time. Months, possibly years. You might want to marry somebody else.'

'I won't.'

'If there's one thing I'm sure of, it's never to be too

sure of anything. Life plays funny tricks. You, if anyone, must know that. If you still feel the same way when I get back, we'll talk again.'

It was less than she wanted, but she knew her own worth and beauty, and replied composedly, 'I'll be waiting. That *is* something you can be sure of, Ben.'

Her lips touched his cheek briefly, as though sealing a bargain rather than promising future passion, and some less disciplined part of his mind wondered if Gary and Joseph had gone to their graves with no warmer memories of her.

Ben came back to the present still wondering about that, and he tried to imagine Linda with her hair loose and dishevelled, her magnolia complexion flushed and her lips parted with desire. It was as difficult as picturing a marble statue come to life, but he had no such trouble when the face of the girl from the store once more intruded with annoying persistence on his thoughts.

She was the very opposite of Linda. Irrational, impetuous, emotional—and Vargas obviously hadn't succeeded in teaching her how a woman should behave, even one who was not a lady. Scratch her, and the savage would show.

It was too late for anybody to do anything about that. Realistically, Ben accepted that the best Vargas could hope for was to cow her by brutality, though he doubted if the trader would hold on to her long enough to succeed. It was more likely that she would pass through many hands, as such girls did, and, unless she had the shrewdness to profit from her beauty while it lasted, her ultimate fate was easy to predict. The time could well come when she remembered the wretched store as something of a haven.

Irritated by finding himself dwelling on how much harsh living it took to turn a lovely young girl into a wrinkled harridan, Ben sought once more for the true reason for his uneasiness.

It all came back to Vargas. For all his smiling servility there had been something almost proprietorial in the way he had studied Ben's possessions. As though he owned them himself, or expected to.

Vargas oozed that combination of cowardice, cunning and covetousness which was a natural breeding-ground for duplicity. He would be able to change his colours with the ease of a chameleon to wring benefit out of any given situation, however discouraging it seemed on the surface.

But Ben found it difficult to see what threat Vargas could pose. If it hadn't been for Clare's ring in his pocket, the fresh supplies on his pack-horse and the searing effect of the hot chilli lingering in his throat, the store and its strange assortment of human beings could well seem no more than a mirage.

For all his musings, Ben had not missed how much the landscape had altered and, with evening approaching, his mind swung from the hypothetical to the practical. Soon he would have to decide whether to camp, or to push on while the light held, to make up for time lost on his detour.

The foothills were rising ever more sharply as they prepared to merge with the mountain looming in gaunt splendour before him, curtailing his freedom of movement and forcing him back to the main trail.

Ben wiped his forehead with his arm, streaking the gritty dust that clung to him like a second skin. Shadows had lengthened into purple pools of mystery as the sun,

its fiery fury almost spent, mellowed into a friend rather
than an enemy.

He dismounted and tied his horses to one of the
gnarled pinion trees that were becoming more frequent
among the scrub and cactus. Unlooping his binoculars
from the high Spanish-style pommel of his saddle and
sliding his rifle from its scabbard, he went ahead on foot
among the rocks veiling the trail.

A breeze blowing down from the mountain carried
with it the refreshing tang of junipers and cedars and he
breathed deeply to rid his lungs of the dusty desert air.
He climbed to a ledge littered with fallen stones and lay
flat to study the meanderings of the trail beside the
stream some three hundred feet below.

A steep grass-covered slope led down to it, but on the
other side there was only vertical rock, as if the matching
slope had been hacked away by a giant sword. The
stream took the line of least resistance round great
clumps of boulders which made a tortuous bottleneck of
the trail and limited his vision in both directions.

Ben frowned and raised his binoculars to study the
mountain, so intent on catching signs of life that he was
blind to the awesome beauty created by the sun as its
waning rays clothed the harsh rock-faces with muted
red.

Only one thing moved. A hawk almost as big as an
eagle was circling slowly on white-barred wings in a
hunger-driven search for snakes. Ben trained his glasses
back the way he had come, and through a gap in the
rocks he thought he saw something else. He watched a
closer gap, and waited.

He was rewarded by a glimpse of a rider which was
sufficient for him to identify the distinctive black and

white markings of a horse he had last seen in the corral at the store and, unless he was very much mistaken, the rider was a woman.

Had the girl been stupid enough to follow him? He swore, for Vargas would be coming after her, and he wanted even less to get involved in their domestic problems on this restricted stretch of trail than he had in the openness of the desert.

Lying flat on the ledge and peering through the cover provided by loosely-piled stones, he had a good view without risking being seen by anybody passing below. Within a short while the horse appeared at a walking pace and, sure enough, the girl was astride him. Her face and hair were hidden by a large black hat, but her clothing was easily identifiable, and so were the bare feet in the stirrups.

Ben swore again, but it didn't relieve his anger. Why, of all the men who must stop at the store, did she have to pick on him? Why not Harry Kirby, who wouldn't have needed asking twice? Fuming, he saw the black hat tilt and then her pale face look upwards, as though she were uneasy. Perhaps, like himself, she found this bottleneck claustrophobic after so much open country.

The girl's back was straight, but there was a droop to her shoulders which suggested that she was wearier than her horse. He watched her rein in and sit motionless, and hoped she was discouraged enough to turn back.

He was right about one thing. Far below him, Sanna *was* weary, but she wasn't discouraged. She was wondering how much more effort she could ask from her horse before letting him rest, as she also longed to do. She was desperately hungry, and for hours she had been mourn-

ing her lost food. Sighing, she decided she must keep
going as long as Magpie could put one foot in front of the
other and the light held, in the diminishing hope she
would overtake Mr Maddox before nightfall.

She touched Magpie gently with her heels and he
gamely began to trot, which she hadn't expected, but she
thought he must be as eager to get out of this spooky
place as she was. She rode round a great outcrop of
boulders and disappeared from the view of the man
quietly cursing her on the ledge. Her hands were slack
on the reins and she gave another of the yawns that were
coming with increasing frequency. Oh, to be safe with
Mr Maddox and for this never-ending day to fade into
merciful night!

That was her last coherent thought before there was a
blur of movement among the rocks and rough hands
dragged her from the saddle. She screamed and struggled as she felt the strength of a man's arm around her
and groped frantically for her knife as she was clamped
against a hard body.

Impressions piled one on the other as her mind
reacted like a kaleidoscope that had been shaken too
swiftly for a pattern to register. She was aware of
another figure jumping in front of the rearing Magpie,
and of the horse bolting back the way they had come;
of grasping her knife and striking wildly with it until
there was a grunt of pain and she was dropped abruptly
on hard pebbles; of grasping a handful and hurling
them with stinging force at the second man coming at
her.

The impressions clarified into the knowledge that she
was being attacked by Manolito and Manuel. Scram-
bling to her feet, tripping and recovering, she fled after

her horse, her skirts held high so that her legs could move freely.

A horrified glance over her shoulder showed Manuel close behind, followed by Manolito who was clutching a bloodstained arm, and she knew with sobbing fear she couldn't outrun them. She veered from the trail and raced up the sandy slope she had just ridden past in an attempt to reach the ledge and hurl stones at them.

It was a forlorn hope, and mixed in with her despair was the agony of knowing that Mr Maddox couldn't have slipped past the Apaches, and that they must have dealt with him in their usual murderous fashion before she had come along.

Sanna was carried a third of the way up the slope by sheer momentum before her feet began to slip. She grabbed at the grass to help her, and that was very nearly her undoing for it was loosely rooted in the sandy soil and came away in her hands.

As she teetered, trying to regain her balance, Manuel grabbed her ankle. Sanna screamed like a trapped animal and threw herself flat, kicking out desperately. She managed to free herself, but she joined Manuel in a dust-choking slide towards the bottom. She clutched without much hope at a clump of grass, and mercifully it held long enough to stop her descent. Once more she started upwards, her breath coming in painful gasps, her strength almost spent.

The sharp crack of a rifle almost caused her labouring heart to stop. Instinctively she threw herself flat and looked round, peering through billowing clouds of dust to see Manolito throw out his arms and collapse backwards. Manuel, his pursuit of her abandoned, was running like a hare for the cover of the rocks.

Almost casually, the rifle sounded again, and she saw Manuel pitch forward on his face. Deafened by the noise and dazed by the suddenness of her deliverance, it took her over-stressed mind long moments to figure out what had happened. Only one solution presented itself. She looked up at the ledge and shouted joyfully, 'Mr Maddox! Mr Maddox!'

He was safe, her special man, and it was a tribute to the depth of her unsolicited feeling for him that her relief was greater on his behalf than on her own.

With renewed energy she again tackled the slope and finally hauled herself triumphantly on to the ledge. She collapsed face down beside him, her shoulders heaving as her lungs gasped for air, too exhausted to do anything but murmur, 'I've found you . . . Glory be, I've found you.'

There couldn't have been more fervour in her voice if she had succeeded in finding the Holy Grail, but he hissed irritably, 'Shut up.' It was the only acknowledgment he gave of her presence, for he was studying the mountain as it returned to its customary brooding silence after the commotion. The hawk had been scared away by the rifle, and the flocks of lesser birds which had risen in shrill alarm were settling down.

Sanna hadn't expected him to be overwhelmed with pleasure at their reunion, even had it taken place under less dramatic circumstances, but her own elation was sufficient to part her lips in a smile that was more than usually dazzling because of her dusty face, as she raised herself weakly to her hands and knees.

All the same she was unprepared as his hand came heavily down on the nape of her neck and her smiling

mouth was filled with grit when he thrust her unceremoniously down into the dirt again, and held her
there.

CHAPTER
SIX

SANNA CHOKED and spluttered, but her indignant squawks were muffled until the pressure eased slightly on her neck and she was able to raise her head sufficiently to exclaim, 'What did you have to do that for? You really are the most cantankerous man!'

'You're the stupidest woman. Stay down. Apaches are harder to spot than lizards among these rocks and I could do without you landing any more on my doorstep.'

'Oh, so that's it,' Sanna replied, relieved that he had a reason for being spiteful—which, with men, wasn't always the case. 'You don't have to worry about more of them. There were only those two, Manolito and Manuel. I know them because they're some kind of cousins of Señora Vargas—nasty murdering brutes always hanging around the store. They were out here waiting for you, but it seems I sprang the trap instead. Vargas arranged it on account of you had things he wanted. I suppose that makes him no better than a murderer himself, not that I ever thought anything different. Mr Maddox, I hate to complain, but do you think you could let me go?'

'You said a lot of things at the store, but you didn't warn me about them.' He sounded surly, but he released her.

Sanna sat up, gingerly massaging her neck where she could still feel the heavy imprint of his hand. 'Vargas told me only after you'd gone. He was gloating about you soon being dead. I was worried silly that you would be, too, unless I reached you in time to warn you.'

'Is that why you came after me?'

Honesty compelled Sanna to admit, 'No, I was coming anyway, though . . .' and try as she might she couldn't stop an aggrieved tone creeping into her voice, 'I did think stopping you riding into an ambush would make you pleased to see me. Still, all's well that ends well, as the great bard said.'

When he stared at her, she explained proudly, 'Shakespeare. I know about him.'

Ben continued to stare. She looked solid enough, all covered in dust though she was and with one white shoulder gleaming through a rent in her blouse where one of the Indians had almost torn the sleeve out, and yet there was something about her which wasn't quite real. If she had been shaking like a leaf or having screaming hysterics she would have seemed normal enough, but she was smiling and chattering as if nearly being captured by a pair of cut-throat Indians was an everyday occurrence. Unless, of course, she was simple-minded. That would explain everything.

It might also make her that much harder to get rid of, which he planned to do at once. Speaking slowly and distinctly so that there could be no chance of her mis-understanding, he said, 'I meant it when I said you couldn't tag along with me. You'd have saved yourself a lot of trouble if you'd listened, so save yourself a whole lot more by listening now. Go after your horse and, when you find him, keep on going until you're home.'

Sanna reached out and clutched his short brown hair, shaking his head affectionately, 'You talk very tough but you don't mean it. You can't, not after I saved you from Manolito and Manuel.'

He knocked her hand away angrily. 'Who saved whom?'

She could see he was still as prickly as a cactus and not at all ready to accept her yet, which saddened her, but she explained patiently, 'They'd have killed you outright, but it wouldn't have made any sense killing me, on account of I'm a young female and beautiful and all. They'd have sold me back to Vargas. They arranged my sale to him in the first place after they'd seen me living with the Apaches that had captured me. It seemed a change for the better, but I was just as much a slave and . . .'

She broke off, wrinkling her straight nose thoughtfully as she sought for words to explain her next predicament, ladylike words that wouldn't embarrass him. 'I was a girl slave with the Apaches, but with Vargas I grew into a woman slave, if you know what I mean, and life got more complicated.'

Ben, looking from her appealing eyes to her even more appealing curves, did know. He also knew that some Indians weren't fussy about waiting for puberty before marrying, and suspected that for all her apparent simplicity she was shrewd enough to cover up a part of her past it was politic to forget. He put her wholesome untouched look down to her youth, and could understand Vargas's eagerness to buy her. She must have made a refreshing change from his repulsive wife, though keeping the peace between the two women couldn't have been easy.

Thinking of the storekeeper prompted Ben to repeat, 'Go home. Vargas will be searching for you. You might meet up with him before dark.'

Sanna's eyes lit with laughter. 'The only thing Vargas will be doing is getting his breath back. I stampeded all his livestock when I escaped, and he must have spent the better part of the afternoon rounding everything up. Glory be, he was as mad as fire and just as hot.' She chuckled at the memory, then added, 'Besides, he won't see any need to chase me. He'll be expecting Manolito and Manuel to bring me in after they've dealt with you. It will be a day or two before he realises you've dealt with them, and he won't have the nerve to chase me then because he'll guess I'm with you.'

As if that was Vargas satisfactorily dealt with, she began to brush the dirt from her clothes with blithe unconcern, pausing only to smile at him trustingly and add, 'You spook him. I don't know why. You don't spook me. I feel safer with you than I've ever felt in my life.'

Ben glared at her. 'You were never less safe, nor are you staying with me. I don't want you.'

Sanna sighed. 'I've been thinking about that. The only sense I can make of it is that you're used to ladies in pretty dresses. You'll just have to imagine how I'll be when I'm dressed properly and my hair's all curled the way it should be. I reckon you'll be wanting to marry me right off, then, just to be sure no other gentleman will get me. What's more, you'll be as proud as a peacock that I'm willing.'

She carefully began smoothing the dust from her cheeks and, misreading the disbelief in his eyes, enlightened him. 'A peacock has the finest feathers that ever grew out of a bird and, my word, how it knows it! It struts around like it's lord of the whole of creation.'

'I know what a damn peacock is,' Ben exploded.

Sanna eyed him warily. She hadn't meant to make him cross and she smiled to placate him. When it didn't seem to be enough, she said, 'Silly me, of course you know about peacocks, you being a proper gentleman as I can tell from your fine horses and things. I mean, even I know and I'm not a proper lady yet. You mustn't go thinking I expect you to strut exactly like one of those birds, because that would be ridiculous. No, I was just trying to make a point. Maybe,' she added uncertainly, her white teeth catching her full lower lip, 'I shouldn't have bothered?'

'My God,' he muttered, 'don't you ever stop talking?'

'I'm starved of somebody to talk to. I hated Vargas, so I never talked to him. Would you like me to shut up?'

'I'd like you to go away.'

'That I can't do, though it pains me not to obey you, because I've set my mind on pleasing you. Which reminds me, I'm not likely to do that if I get freckles on my face, am I? I must find my hat. I lost it when Manolito leapt out at me.'

Ben's frustration was mounting with every nonsensical thing she said. He had one last try at getting through to her. 'Vargas might not be much, but you have a good chance of staying alive with him. With me you have hardly any. I'm after a murderer, and he knows it, so the odds are stacked in his favour. I've no time to spend fussing around a girl. If he gets me and you're not killed outright, he'll take you for his woman, and that won't be any picnic. When he tires of you he'll toss you to his men as if you're no more than a scrap from last night's supper.

Do you get that?' When Sanna nodded, he snapped, 'Good. Now go home.'

She didn't stir. 'I'm truly sorry you've got trouble, Mr Maddox, but I don't mean to add to it. I mean to help any way I can. Now don't go getting cross for no reason, because the truth is I'd rather die now than go back to Vargas. You've warned me fair and square, and I understand that it won't be your fault if something bad happens to me.'

'You don't understand,' he said angrily. 'You only think you do.'

'I understand that whatever happens to me from now on will be from my own doing. I've never had a choice before, not in my whole life, not about anything. You have to be a prisoner to know how important that is.' Sanna's voice quivered. She brought it under control and added resolutely, 'My choice—my first free choice—is to be with you. I don't want to die, and I don't expect to because I'm amazingly good at surviving, but . . .' Her voice trailed away.

'But what?' he asked harshly, the question coming out against his will.

'But if it does happen, will you bury me properly? If peacocks are the prettiest birds, vultures must be the ugliest.' She looked up at the big ragged-winged birds which had appeared from nowhere to circle above the bodies of Manolito and Manuel, shuddered, and clutched Ben's sleeve. 'I've always had a terrible fear of them getting me. If you promise me a good deep grave should I be unlucky enough to need one, I promise in my turn that I won't ask you for another thing—not even the silk dress I'm just about busting my sides to get.'

The effect of this touching little speech was to harden,

if possible, Ben's resistance to her. The offer of her body having failed to snare him, he decided she was trying the more subtle appeal of words. She must think he was still naïve enough to cherish chivalrous notions about women, which was her mistake, while his had been to listen to her for too long. To convince her once and for all that she was not travelling with him, he dispensed with words altogether and thrust her off the ledge.

Sanna, taken unawares, yelped and became a flailing bundle of arms and legs as she tumbled over and over until she reached the bottom. The vultures sheered off in alarm as she shook her dazed head, crawled sideways out of the dust-cloud she had created, and got to her feet.

She wasn't used to gentle treatment, nor had anybody ever considered her dignity, but her fists clasped in exasperation as she looked up at Ben and shouted, 'If you had any sense you'd be fighting to get at me, not get rid of me. I'm beautiful, for heaven's sake, if you'd only stop rolling me in the dust long enough for my face to show through!'

She marched up the slope with such grim determination that she managed it more easily than her previous attempts. She hauled herself on to the ledge, sat down, and said with all the dogged defiance in her nature, 'We can keep this up all night and it won't make any difference. I've set my mind on staying with you, and stay I will. If you beat me into the ground I'll just get back up and come on after you.' She puffed out her cheeks and released her pent-up feelings in a noisy sigh as if that finished the matter, which, for her, it did.

Ben didn't doubt it. For the moment he was beaten, a

novel experience which didn't make him feel any more kindly disposed towards her. Simple-minded was bad enough but stubborn was worse. She was a nuisance and would never be anything else for, as she so vainly kept pointing out, she was beautiful. Men he had no quarrel with would try to pick one on her account, and he had trouble enough.

It would take a man of stone not to touch her, yet, if he did, she would become even more impossible to get rid of. Like ivy, she would cling. And also, like ivy, there was a strong chance that she would destroy whatever she clung to—unless she was destroyed first.

Whichever way he looked at it he didn't want to be involved, but from the passive way she was regarding him, full of the stoic fatalism of a dog that knew it was about to be kicked, he realised he was stuck with her until he could offload her on some man she saw as a better prospect. For a few baubles, the silk dress she had been babbling about, she would be anybody's.

'All right,' he said reluctantly. 'You can stay with me . . .'

With a gasp of delight Sanna flung her arms around his neck and hugged him, choking off the rest of his words. She hadn't dared to hope he would capitulate without her first taking more punishment, and she was too unsophisticated to contain her joy. She was rather like the dog he had privately likened her to, so starved of any person on which to lavish the love in her generous heart that it all poured out of her at the least sign of encouragement.

Ben irritably disentangled himself and pushed her away, treatment that didn't seem to surprise her or lessen her happiness. She gazed at him adoringly, fidgeting as she tried to suppress her excitement, and if he had been less cynical and suspicious he would have been flattered that she'd singled him out to be her own particular god. He began again, 'You can stay with me until we come across the first fellow who is willing to take you off my hands. That's all I'm offering. Understood?'

Sanna nodded vigorously, her eyes shining. She felt quite safe in agreeing to his terms, so sure was she that they belonged together and that he would swiftly come to realise it. Then he wouldn't be able to bear giving her away. He would fight to keep her, she thought confidently, just as she would fight to keep him.

'Another thing, I'm not a damned nursemaid,' he was telling her. 'I've got no time to waste. If you can't keep up, you get left behind. I don't want any weeping or wailing. Just fix it in your head right now that although we'll be travelling together I won't be responsible for you.'

'I'm never sick,' she boasted, 'and my horse can keep on going for ever. I'll get him. He won't be far, not being skittish like some.'

Sanna jumped to her feet and bounded down the slope with all the friskiness of a healthy young deer, her fatigue forgotten. After a few minutes she found Magpie placidly cropping grass, and he nuzzled her as she made a fuss of him.

Ben was waiting with his horses when she rode back, and he handed her the leading rein of the pack-horse. 'You might as well make yourself useful. I'll ride behind you so that any more surprises those rocks might be hiding can fall on you rather than me.'

Sanna hadn't expected to be pampered, but she felt she'd had more than her share of rough usage for one day. She didn't want to anger him, so she confined her objection to a mild, 'That hardly seems fair.'

'It isn't, but you might as well understand straight away that my neck is more important to me than yours. You invited yourself along, and that means doing as you're told without argument. If it doesn't suit you, you're welcome to go home.'

Any hopes he had that his words might push some sense into her mule-brained head were dashed when she merely sighed and began to lead the way through the massive boulders. She dismounted swiftly to retrieve her hat when she reached the place of ambush, then quickened the pace until they were through the tortuous bottleneck, and the whole panorama of the mountain unfolded before them.

She felt truly, wonderfully, free at last. No more being constantly on the watch for Vargas's groping hands, no more daily fear that his son would return, or that she would shrivel and die in the desert without ever having really lived.

When Ben took over the lead, her happiness found an outlet in a song she had learned from the Apaches. It seemed in tune with her feelings but it was the only thing that was; Sanna, for all her beauty, sang off key.

Ben's head came round sharply. 'Stop that wailing.'

'I'm happy,' she explained, which didn't increase his estimation of her intelligence, but she dutifully fell silent, her eyes never leaving his straight back so that she could be ready with a smile when he glanced behind.

Magpie broke the silence next with a soft whinny which was answered from behind a thicket of thorn-bushes. Ben investigated, and found Manuel and Manolito's camp, their horses tethered to a rope strung

between two trees. He turned them loose, outraging
Sanna's thrifty soul, for, as she pointed out, 'Those are
good horses. You must be rich enough to buy a mine to
chase off ready cash like that.'

'I'm not a damned trader,' he answered contemptuously, and rode on.

Sanna marvelled at his arrogance, convinced she had
picked a real gentleman for herself, and visions of all the
luxuries she craved floated before her eyes while Ben's
were more practically occupied in searching for a good
place to camp.

He chose a rough circle of rocks not far from the
stream, where there was good grazing for the horses. It
was none too soon, for the reds and purples of the
mountain were dwindling into the anonymous grey of
twilight.

Ben and Sanna were silent was they busied themselves
caring for the horses and setting up camp, Ben because
he was naturally uncommunicative and Sanna because
she was obsessed with the need to eat.

She gathered all the wood she could find in the
fast-fading light, and by the time she had found the
vestas among his supplies and had the fire going it was
dark. As the fragrance of burning sage and pinion
drifted over the campsite, she confessed, 'I lost my
supplies getting away from Vargas. I'll have to share
yours. I'm sorry about that, after promising not to be a
bit of trouble and all.'

Ben was on his way to the stream to wash and didn't
bother to answer, so she took that as permission to cook
enough of his food for two.

By the time he returned, the mouth-watering aromas
of fried strips of pork, coffee and beans were mingling

with the homely smell of woodsmoke. Sanna's hunger was close to pain. It said much for her adoration of Ben that she hadn't stolen any morsels while she cooked and that she willingly piled the larger portion on his plate.

Her own she ate straight from the pans, tossing strips of pork from hand to hand until they cooled sufficiently to hold properly, then crunching them with noisy relish. When the meat was finished, she started on the beans, scooping them into her mouth and sucking her fingers afterwards.

She was so blissfully absorbed in taking the urgent edge from her hunger that it was some time before she became aware that Ben was watching her over the rosy glow of the fire. 'You eat like an animal,' he said disgustedly. 'Don't you have a fork?'

Sanna was surprised. Nobody had ever taught her manners or complained at her lack of them. When she shook her head, he rummaged among his supplies and threw a spare fork at her. She caught it and began to eat with more restraint, copying him. When there wasn't a bean left, she sighed and generously offered the pan to him. 'Would you like to lick this out?'

'Christ, no!'

She blinked at his contempt, for she regarded the pan as the best part, and with her tongue and fingers she searched for the last of the juices, finally stretching her tongue as far as it would go to lick her mouth clean. Convinced at last there wasn't a scrap left, she stretched with the air of one who has dined well and has no further quarrel with the world.

The rising moon was lightening the darkness and casting a silver sheen over everything as her eyes met his.

Her ready smile faded as he said, 'Eat away from me in future. You make me feel ill.'

Dismay filled Sanna. She hadn't expected praise for the quick and tasty meal she had produced, for that was a woman's job, but she had expected his mood to mellow. She poured him a mug of coffee, then another, waiting patiently for her turn.

When he put down the mug and stood up, she seized it and filled it, blowing on the coffee and sipping the scalding liquid noisily. 'Grief,' Ben muttered and walked away.

Sanna began to perceive that there was more to being a lady than wearing a silk dress and having a complexion that wasn't spoiled by the sun, and that a gentleman took more pleasing than ordinary men. She must watch him carefully and learn from him so that she didn't offend him again.

She gathered up the dishes and carried them to the stream to wash, and when she returned he was setting out his bedroll. Sanna stood quite still, and for the first time in that traumatic day her courage deserted her.

It was one thing to accept that the price of her freedom was to lie under a blanket with a man, but quite another to be on the threshold of paying her dues. She began to tremble and wonder what on earth she had done.

CHAPTER
SEVEN

WITH SICKENING clarity Sanna's own words came back to mock her. 'I won't scream or fight or cause you any fuss. We'll be fine together.'

She was anything but fine! She was afraid to move in case she drew attention to herself and had to back up her bold statement. In the silence of the camp her mind seemed to be screaming, *Not now. It's too soon. We're still strangers. I was so desperate back there at the store I didn't know what I was saying. I only thought I did . . .*

Slowly, silently, she put down the pans she had washed. She would creep away until she could find the courage to face that waiting blanket. She was backing away stealthily when Ben said, without turning his head, 'Time to stop fidgeting about and turn in. It will be a long hard ride tomorrow with no store to break the monotony of it.'

'I . . . I . . .' Sanna's voice had vanished with her courage. She cleared her throat and tried again. 'I like to wash before I sleep. A habit, you know, I never break for anything. I . . . I won't be long.'

He stood up and came towards her in his purposeful way. Sanna's trembling legs stiffened into petrified blocks, making flight impossible. She felt as helpless as a rabbit mesmerised by a wolf, terrified by its fate but unable to do anything about it.

Her heart pounded as he reached her, then he brushed past and began kicking sand over the dying embers of the fire. Immeasurable relief flooded through her, bringing some quivering mobility back to her legs. It was only a reprieve, but she must use it to reconcile herself to the menace of that blanket.

She snatched her clean blouse and hairbrush from her bundle, took his towel and soap from the rock as she passed it, and tried to look unconcerned as she went down to the stream. With every step she scolded herself. His opinion of her was low enough already. What would he think if he discovered she was afraid to perform that most necessary of a woman's duties when she picked herself a man? And how could she run away when she had spent the day running after him?

He had made it plain enough that he regarded her as a nuisance, and after all her brazen talk and posturings she would sink to the level of a lying coward. Another Vargas, feminine version.

Sanna recoiled from that as instinctively as she had recoiled from the blanket, and when she reached the stream she was in a flat despair. He was such a cold and controlled man, and she lived by reacting to the emotion of the moment. How could she explain her fears in a way he would understand, always assuming he would be patient enough to listen?

It would be easier, she thought wretchedly as she wandered along the edge of the stream, if she were totally ignorant of what happened between a man and a woman. The fact was that living in the curtained-off storeroom next to the Vargas's bedroom for two years had left her with precious few illusions.

No matter how deeply she had burrowed under her blanket, or how hard she had pressed her hands to her ears, she had been unable to help eavesdropping. What she had heard revolted her and bore no relation to the love she felt for Mr Maddox. That was a thing of the heart, or perhaps the soul, for what other explanation could there be for the instant affinity she had felt?

It was all too new and complex for Sanna to understand herself. All she knew was the love she felt for Mr Maddox was a fine and noble thing, to be nurtured and cherished, and it saddened her that it must be sullied by the animal coupling so essential to men.

For her part, it was enough to be with him, to hug him when she was overwhelmed by one of those rushes of affection he inspired in her, to admire the leanness of his body and the weather-honed features of his face, to gaze as often as she could into his compelling eyes. All these things she relished, but that still left her far short of being ready to sleep under his blanket.

Sanna was as much confused as frightened. It baffled her that she could be so happy with him one moment and want to run away from him the next. It would baffle him, too—and disgust him. She must avoid that at all cost.

The moon was illuminating the stream a little too brightly for Sanna's comfort and she didn't stop walking until she found a rock large enough to shield her from the camp. This, also, was habit and it was instilled in her through the constant need to avoid Vargas's prying eyes.

She took off her torn and travel-stained blouse and anchored it with a stone in the stream so that the dirt would loosen while she washed herself. She soaped her face and shoulders and breasts and tried to banish her girlish fears by reminding herself that she had forced herself on Mr Maddox, not the other way round. It was a pity he hadn't been entranced by his first glimpse of her, as she had always imagined in her dreams, but that made it all the more necessary that she should satisfy his manly needs. He would never fall in love with her if she shrank from him, and then how could she complain if he carried out his threat to pass her on to another man?

Sanna's fantasies about her future had been so rosy that she hadn't considered the possibility of having a baby before she got her fine home. She couldn't help considering it, now that reality was proving to have little in common with her obliging imaginings, and found it a daunting prospect.

Since she knew of no way of avoiding such an occurrence, she supposed she must accept it. No, she chided herself, she must do better than that. She must welcome it. Men despised barren women, and a child as handsome as she and Mr Maddox were likely to make couldn't fail to raise his estimation of her.

Sanna, rinsing off the soap and rubbing herself dry with the towel, had reached that point of passively accepting the inevitable which had seen her through so many of the traumas in her life. A certain peace filled her, enabling the practical side of her nature to reassert itself.

She had no proper drawers, so she took off the baggy cotton peasant's trousers she used as a substitute and washed them with her blouse. She lifted her skirt, quickly washed the rest of her body and put on her clean blouse, her movements becoming more flurried in case Mr Maddox came to see what was keeping her.

She unbraided and brushed her hair, tying it back

loosely with the string which usually secured the plait. She was as ready as she was ever going to be. She gathered up her things and hurried up to the camp.

He was standing by his blanket in his shirt and trousers, boots and gun-belt removed, and he seemed a dark and towering figure to Sanna as she hastily spread out her washing on the rock to dry.

Then she picked up her blanket and walked fatalistically towards him, kneeling to spread it next to his. She had mastered her fear, but there was little she could do about the nervousness that made her fingers fumble or the shyness that kept her head bowed.

When she stood up she hesitated before turning towards him, wishing he would say something kind or gentle—anything that would make her feel it was her, Sanna, he wanted and not just any woman.

She was caught off guard when he grasped her arm and spun her towards him. She gasped and flinched, unprepared for violence if she didn't oppose him. Just as suddenly, she was released. She stumbled, caught her foot in the blanket and sat down unceremoniously.

She stared up at him with fear-widened eyes, imagining what he would do, and saw with disbelief that he had taken the knife from her belt and was sliding it under his blanket. 'What did you do that for?' she demanded.

'I don't trust women.' Ben cocked his rifle and laid it carefully beside his blanket, as he had been taught as a young boy by his father when they were spending the night outside the safety of the *hacienda*. 'There's often only a second or two between life and death, so always give yourself an edge,' Thomas had said, and drove home this and other lessons by making his sons witness the grisly results of unwariness.

'Don't . . . don't trust women,' Sanna burst out. 'You must have maggots in your brain. What do you think I was going to do with that knife? Stick it in you while you were asleep? That's just the sort of thing I would do, isn't it, after going through so much trouble to join up with you!'

'There's no telling what a woman will do.'

Before Sanna's indignant gaze he lay down and covered himself with a blanket, closing his eyes and apparently losing all interest in her. 'Talk about adding insult to injury,' she raved. 'You act like I'm no better than a murdering Indian and won't even stay awake long enough to justify yourself. You call me uncivilised! Well, I'd like to know what you are, grabbing me like that. If you wanted my knife you just had to ask. There was no need to scare me half to death. I declare, one more scare today and I'll faint clean away.'

'I wish you would,' Ben muttered, turning his back on her.

Sanna eyed him balefully and grumbled on. 'I'm surprised you dare take your eyes off me. I might smash your head in with a rock or strangle you with the string I tie up my hair with. My word, there's no end to the evil things I could get up to, me being so untrustworthy and all.'

Provoking no response, she changed tactics. 'Why don't you trust me? What reason have I given you for . . .'

'Don't whine,' he growled.

Sanna's mouth shut with a frustrated snap. She hadn't got through half her grievances, but it was dawning on her that, after she had nerved herself to accept his lovemaking, he hadn't any intention of touching her.

A short while ago she might well have collapsed with relief, but now it was just so much fuel to the fire of her resentment. She was washed, her hair was brushed and she was willing—sort of. She lifted a lock of hair from her shoulder and stared at it. The moonlight had transformed its fairness to shimmering silver and she guessed she must look as near a fairy princess as made no difference.

No matter how lovely she looked or how hard she tried to please him, he had no value for her. Not even trust! Pique sent her off on a tangent, and she fumed, 'Do you know something? You haven't so much as asked my name!'

There was no answer, and she demanded, 'Would you like to know?'

'No. Go to sleep.'

'Well!' Sanna flounced under her blanket, turned her back as pointedly as his was turned to her, and hunched her shoulder as if daring him to touch her now.

He didn't try, and her anger, lacking fuel, began to drain away, allowing a fresh spectre to torment her seething brain. How was she going to make him fall in love with her if he continued to show no inclination to make love *to* her? For all her tacit agreement, she could never allow herself to be passed on to another man.

Sanna turned restlessly on to her back, staring up at the stars and thinking they were no more remote than the man who lay beside her. What could she do that she hadn't done already? She didn't know. The sad fact was that, having spent her years at the store vigilantly avoiding rape, she had learned none of the skills of seduction.

There was no denying that her first try at tempting Mr Maddox so that she could escape from the store had been a dismal failure, and this evening she had been hampered by fear or shyness. Unable to decide what to do next, it suddenly bothered her very much that he didn't know her name. They had started the day as strangers, they mustn't finish it so.

She propped herself up on her elbow and gently touched his shoulder. 'It's Sanna,' she whispered. 'My name is Sanna.'

He didn't answer, and there was no telling whether he was asleep or merely ignoring her. Disappointed, she lay down. The weariness that had been held at bay by the excitement of finding him and being allowed to stay with him now began to lull her over-active mind.

One of the last thoughts she had was that if he was the most unsociable of men, she must be the most contrary of women. Lying quietly beside him like this she felt no fear, only a rather wistful need to touch him.

She inched stealthily towards his still frame until her cheek rested against his back. It was the lightest of contacts, but it must have provided the reassurance she craved, for she fell instantly into a deep and dreamless sleep.

It was barely light when Sanna opened her eyes to find that Ben had gone. She sat up, wide awake, filled with alarm that he had slipped off during the night and left her. Then one of the shadows moved slightly and she released her pent-up breath in a whoosh of relief. He was still there, though for some reason incomprehensible to her he had moved his bedroll during the night.

She was too inexperienced to realise that though his body next to hers had been a great comfort, hers had had the reverse effect on him. Ben had found rest impossible until he'd moved away, and even then his sleep had been fitful. Her proximity appeared to have the power to disturb even his unconscious mind.

Time and again during the night his eyes had opened and sought her sleeping form, and the thought of suffering through a string of similar nights before he could get rid of her brought a scowl to his face as he watched her get up. He wondered if he was being unnecessarily cautious in keeping his hands off her, and yet his instinct persisted in drumming out the message that she would be twice as troublesome if he allowed himself to become more deeply involved.

As for Sanna, when she stood up and wrapped her shawl around her, her mood was at its sunniest best. The trials and tribulations of the previous day might never have happened. Another day was always, for her, another chance. She built a new fire from the wood left over from the night before with nothing heavier on her mind than getting breakfast ready before Mr Maddox awoke.

When the fire was going, she tied back her hair with string, meaning to brush and braid it later, quite unaware he was watching her every move—or that his resentment of her flared anew when he realised he was behaving no better than a peeping Tom.

The first intimation she had that he was awake was when he flung his blanket aside. The pale oval of her face turned towards him as she scolded cheerfully, 'If it isn't just like you to wake up too soon. I was hoping to have your breakfast all ready for you, but don't fret, I'll rush the coffee and you can enjoy that while the food is cooking.'

'Don't fuss,' he snapped, pulling on his boots and uncocking his rifle now that the night was safely over.

'Glory be, what a man you are for "dont's". Don't talk, don't whine, don't fuss,' she chided him, but playfully, for there was great joy for her in being with him and not at the store preparing for another depressing day of watching Vargas watching her, and his wife blearily watching them both.

Sanna, bustling around the fire, glanced over her shoulder in time to see him walking away with his binoculars in one hand and his rifle in the other. She sighed but refused to be discouraged. He could hardly expect to remain a stranger for another day. She simply wouldn't let him.

Dawn was clawing its way across the sky with pale pink fingers as Ben made his way out of camp and climbed to a vantage-point, barely giving sufficient light for him to study the terrain ahead, but he wanted to get away from the girl for a while. He raised his binoculars and swept the landscape with professional thoroughness, assessing it as dispassionately as he assessed his unwanted companion.

She was iike a burr in his side, prickling and pestering for attention he didn't want to give. She was behaving as if they were on a picnic, yet she must be as aware as himself how hostile this territory was.

She seemed to live by the minute, trusting to providence to deliver her from evil. Ben had no such trust, and nothing she had said or done had altered his opinion that she was an unnecessary hazard. She stumbled mindlessly from one predicament to another and, as though that wasn't enough, her sensuality was bidding to become a major torment.

He wondered how soon he would be able to leave her, and the prospects weren't encouraging. The mountains were gouged by spectacular canyons, some of which it could take days to cross, hard days of balancing on trails so sheer that they were barely climbable. They would pass isolated dwellings, poor and prosperous villages, and perhaps in some sheltered valley a *hacienda* as proud and rich as his own home.

Not exactly an ideal dumping-ground for a young American girl, Ben thought bitterly, but she did have considerable beauty to recommend her. She might even be lucky and end up with more silk dresses than she could wear, if she lived long enough.

Ben remembered her boasting how strong and healthy she was, but it took toughness and cunning to survive a territory which had plenty of natural hazards to discourage travellers. Add to that the ever-present risk of bandits and roving bands of Indians, the certainty of a confrontation with Harry Kirby, and the sooner he could be rid of her, the better it would be for her as well as himself.

He had left the camp because of the girl, and it was the smell of her cooking that drew him back. His restless night made him feel as if it was a long time since he had eaten.

Sanna began to serve as soon as she glimpsed him, handing him his plate and mug of coffee as he sat across the fire from her, with an apologetic, 'The same as supper, I'm afraid, but it will be good for all that. I could have made tortillas if we'd had any flour. We'll get some the first place we come to.'

'The first place we come to is likely to be the last place we'll be together,' he told her, irritated that with her hair tousled from sleep and tied back anyhow she still managed to look fresh and enticing.

To his surprise, she grinned. 'You'll have to stop being so welcoming. It might go to my head and there'll be no doing anything with me.'

'You'll be strangled with your own tongue one of these days,' he prophesied. 'Where are you going to eat?'

'Right here, but you don't have to worry. I'm waiting until everything cools so that I can be as dainty as you are.'

'I am not dainty,' he exploded.

'You're not any sweeter tempered in the morning than you are at night, either,' she chided him cheerfully. 'And that reminds me. I couldn't find any sugar in your supplies last night. I meant to ask whether you don't like it or whether you forgot to order some at the store.'

'I don't forget things.'

'So you don't like it. Pity, because I'm partial to it myself, but I'll learn to manage without it. I don't want you buying anything especially for me, although with me not being a slave any more and expected to work for nothing, you could say I was paying my way by doing the cooking and washing. Which also reminds me—give me your dirty clothes at night and I'll wash them with mine.'

'I'm not helpless.'

Sanna sighed. 'Maybe you should try sugar with your coffee. It might sweeten you up a little. It puzzles me, Mr Maddox, what you've got against me.'

'At the store, nothing. Here, everything.'

'It must be nice to have your food cooked for you,' she coaxed.

'I'd swop it for some peace and quiet.'

She pulled a very unladylike face but said no more, not because she was discouraged but because she had to concentrate on the monumental task of eating without offending him. She took finicky little bites from her meat, chewed with her mouth shut, and if she wasn't rewarded with compliments, at least she earned no scowls or bitter remarks.

She watched him avidly, thinking it must take a lot of practice to eat as fast and as tidily as he did. For her part, she felt she had never worked so long and hard to get her food to her stomach.

She was learning how to get a forkful of beans to her mouth without dropping any, instead of leaning over the pan and scooping them in any whichway, when he suddenly said, 'Sanna. That's a hell of a name. What's it short for?'

So he *had* been listening last night and he *was* interested in her! Sanna's eyes glowed like sapphires as tears of joy welled up and spilled over. She didn't seem to notice, and quite forgot her manners as she answered eagerly, 'That's a puzzle, Mr Maddox, a real puzzle, and I'm never going to be sure of the solution. I was so young when Mr Blakeney bought me I could only call myself Sanna, so everybody called me that, too, and it stuck. I reckon it must have been Susanna once and . . .'

'Don't talk with your mouth full,' Ben interrupted, her overflow of emotion, for no reason that he could deduce, confirming his suspicions that she wasn't quite right in the head.

'Oh!' She swallowed with guilty haste, choked, and had a coughing fit which brought tears of a different kind to her eyes. As soon as she could, she resumed undaunted, '. . . and I'd be as pleased as a dog with two tails, both of them wagging, if you could see your way to calling me Susanna. It's a bit of a mouthful . . .' she touched her throat and laughed, 'just like those beans I swallowed too fast, but it's much grander than Sanna, and I intend to be very grand.'

Holy smoke, Ben thought, asking her a simple question was like taking the top off a geyser and being drowned in a gush of words. He hadn't even meant to ask the question. It had asked itself. He would have to watch that no more did. The slightest bit of encouragement, and she was swift to involve him in her life, giving him that ivy feeling he abhorred.

Sanna's pause was to give him time to enquire who Mr Blakeney was. When he didn't, she told him anyway. 'I guess you'd call Mr Blakeney a pedlar, though he was an actor at one time, which is how I came to know about Shakespeare. He used to give poetry readings if people paid him, which they very often did—being hungry, as he said, for culture. Mostly, though, he made his money selling medicine and hardware and haberdashery and whatever else he could cram into the wagon. We travelled all over the place, just like gipsies, which is why I'm never too sure where I've been or what I saw where. It was confusing, you know?'

When Ben refused to be drawn, she refilled his coffee mug and chattered on. 'I had my own tray of ribbons and brooches and such stuff to sell. I had a pink silk dress and pink ribbons in my hair because he said women would buy stuff to make their daughters look just like me, and if they didn't have any, they'd buy stuff anyway on account of I was so sweet.'

Sanna laughed and leaned over the fire to push his shoulder playfully. 'In some places, can you believe, I used to sell my whole trayful and have to stock up again! Only, a good day's trading meant a hard night's drinking for Mr Blakeney. I didn't care for that too much because that's when he really went to town on Shakespeare, ranting on so that a body couldn't get any sleep. He always told the customers I was his poor motherless daughter, and that's what I believed for years until he got a different sort of drunk one night and told me my real story. He said I was a love-child and my mother had left me at a Kentucky farm when I was a baby. When I was about three, the money for my keep stopped coming, so the farmer's wife traded me to Mr Blakeney for a length of calico and half a dozen knives and forks. He thought I'd bring in trade, and so I did. She told him she had too many children of her own to feed and I was nothing but a love-child nobody wanted.'

Her chin lifted defiantly. 'I didn't let that get me down. I figured if I was pretty enough to sell stuff to people, I was pretty enough for somebody to want some day—and I didn't even know I was going to grow so beautiful then. It used to sadden me that, when we weren't selling, Mr Blakeney made me pack away my silk dress and ribbons and put on dowdy old cotton like I'm wearing now. Lordy, how he used to scold every time I grew out of a dress! He said women wouldn't be such a soft touch if I got gawky and he'd have to get another little girl to take my place, only that never happened because . . .'

Sanna's runaway tongue came up against a memory that effectively tied it in knots. She said, after an awkward pause Ben did nothing to fill, 'Listen to me, rattling on. Have you finished with your mug, Mr Maddox?'

Ben wondered what incident she had recalled which had stopped her dead, when she seemed set to keep going until supper time. Seduction? Rape? Something she wasn't willing to talk about, anyhow. He stopped speculating, handed her the mug and stood up. 'We'll break camp as soon as this lot's cleared away.'

Sanna nodded, thinking that in a better world bad things from the past wouldn't reach out to spoil the happiness of the present. She poured herself coffee, grimaced at its bitterness, and said, 'Mr Maddox, since you know I'm Sanna, and maybe Susanna if it pleases you, do you think I could know your first name?'

'Maddox will do,' he told her.

'But I've told you a lot about me, and it's such a tiny thing to tell me about yourself.'

Ben turned away. 'Save all your questions for the next man you latch on to. You know as much about me now as you're ever going to know.'

CHAPTER
EIGHT

THEY HAD been riding for several hours, and Ben had decided long since that Sanna was the noisiest creature he had ever come across. If she wasn't singing or whistling, she was talking. Under different circumstances he might have enjoyed listening to her speak, for her voice had a musical Mississippi lilt—unlike her off-key singing and whistling—but she exasperated him by jumping inconsequentially from one subject to another, all of them irrelevant.

He tried to stay out of earshot, but she and her comic-opera horse, with its black head and black-splotched white body, were never more than a few paces behind. The respites he gained by snubbing her into silence never lasted long. No sooner had his nerves unjangled than she would start singing or whistling again. Softly at first, then more boldly, and finally she would bombard him with questions which he welcomed as much as the insects which pestered him from time to time. He answered none of them, but that didn't deter her.

She was like a cock that wouldn't stop crowing until somebody wrung its neck. Apparently she was unaware of how his strong fingers itched to do just that, because she was asking, 'Why don't horses have horns like goats and cows? I wonder if they can think about things like that? It must be terrible not to be able to think. It passes the time so much. Is that why you're so quiet, Mr Maddox, because you're always thinking?'

Ben glanced back, but not to answer her question or her hopeful smile. It was a matter of habit, checking the trail behind to make sure he wasn't being followed, and Sanna had become accustomed to his eyes staring past her as though she were invisible. This time, however, she rated a long hard stare.

'What, in the name of—! You look like a damned vulture!' he exclaimed.

Sanna giggled. The sun was still climbing to its zenith and as soon as she'd felt the heat of its angled rays on her cheek and neck she'd fished her piece of black lace from her bundle. She'd tied it over the crown of her floppy hat so that its soft folds fell protectively to her shoulders. She lifted the lace to grin mischievously at him. 'Don't you fret, I'm under here all right. Just me. No freckles or nasty blotches from insect bites.'

She let the lace fall back, and continued, 'It's a real pride having a pale skin, but such a pain keeping it nice. You've no notion! Just look how brown my hands are. Not like a lady's at all. One day I'm going to have gloves to keep them white. Silk gloves, like my dress and cushion.'

Ben asked unguardedly, 'Cushion?'

'Cushion,' she reiterated firmly, encouraged enough to urge Magpie and the pack-horse she was leading alongside his. The stream was several hundred feet below them to their right, idling its way along the shadowed bottom of a forbidding ravine, but to their left the mountain rose gently so that there was ample room.

'Just because I've been living at the tail end of nowhere doesn't mean I'm totally ignorant.'

She raised the lace again to look challengingly at him, but when he made no comment she dropped it, and added, 'Not about ladies, anyway. They have pale skins and wear silk dresses and live in great white houses. The really grand ladies throw silk cushions on the grass to sit on. They're so rich they don't have to fret about the silk spoiling, which I wouldn't believe at all if I hadn't seen them for myself, so you can tell why I need a silk cushion.'

With the lace shrouding her face, Ben couldn't see her expression, but her tone told him she believed every incredible word she said. He said flatly, 'All the silk cushions in the world wouldn't make a lady out of you.'

'Why not? You can tell ladies by the things they have. I just need the right things.'

'There's a lot more to it than that. Ladies come from good families and they marry into good families. You don't have any kind of family, and with your kind of past, marriage is out.'

'What's wrong with my past?'

'You've lived with Indians and a Mexican.'

'It's not fair to blame me for what I couldn't help,' Sanna pointed out reasonably.

'Maybe not, but if you go back over the border you'll find yourself an outcast among your own people. Women who are captured by Indians are supposed to kill themselves. Didn't you know that?'

'No, and I'm glad I didn't. What a dumb thing to do when there's always a chance of being traded on or escaping,' Sanna retorted.

Ben felt that, as usual with her, she was missing the

point. He told her bluntly, because she had to learn some time, 'You're not respectable, and if a woman isn't respectable she can't be a lady. You heard the saying that you can't make a silk purse out of a sow's ear? Well, that's what I mean. Real ladies will never accept you. They'll peck you to pieces.'

'Is that so?' Sanna demanded, lifting her veil to reveal blazing blue eyes. 'They'd better watch out, that's all I can say. I can do a fine bit of pecking myself.'

'You won't get the chance, because you won't find a man to marry you, not the kind you're after.'

Sanna thought that over, then said, 'You're forgetting something, Mr Maddox. What you say may hold true for plain girls, but I'm beautiful. I'll get what I want, you'll see.'

Ben gave up. She was never going to see sense until her nose was rubbed in it. As for Sanna, nothing could shift from her head the conviction that when he saw her dressed as a lady he would accept her as one. She blamed his present prejudices on her dreary outgrown cotton clothes. In her mind's eye she saw a silk dress as something of a magic wand, transforming her and making her wholly desirable as a gentleman's wife.

Of course, it would help if she could speed the process by making him fall in love with her first. She looked at his profile, her eyes lingering on his straight strong nose, his firm lips and chin, and the wave of adoration that swept over her was so fierce that it was akin to pain. It still didn't seem right that she could feel so much for him without him feeling anything in return, but since she was naïve enough to believe right had to triumph in the end, she assured herself it was only a matter of time.

They rested the horses in the shade of a cluster of

pinion trees during the worst heat of the day, eating strips of dried meat and drinking the tepid water they carried with them. Sanna fell asleep and had to be shaken awake when it was time to ride on.

They were climbing ever higher, and Ben looked behind so many times that Sanna found herself glancing back, too, but she saw nothing and gave up, content to let Ben be cautious enough for both of them. Towards evening what had been a pleasant breeze increased in velocity, whipping at their hats and ponchos and lashing the dry earth into dust devils which leaped and spun from slope to slope.

Even so, Sanna was surprised how early Ben stopped to camp. She was also delighted. Not only was she ravenous, she was unused to long hours in the saddle and her very bones seemed to ache from weariness.

The site Ben chose was well screened from the wind by thick bushes and a stand of juniper and pinion trees. A narrow stream lazed its way through the trees as though it scarcely had the strength to trickle over the ravine a couple of hundred yards away.

As soon as the horses were cared for, Ben took his rifle and binoculars and disappeared, without a word as usual. Sanna sighed as she gathered wood and lit a fire. If the end of the day wasn't the time to talk, when was? She checked her critical thoughts, blaming them on hunger, and while she cooked she wondered why she was always hungry.

She hoped it wasn't because she was still growing. She had lost her gawky look when her breasts and hips had plumped out, and she had a fear of becoming lanky. She was already tall for a woman, and although Mr Maddox was tall for a man, she liked the way she didn't quite top his shoulders. It made such a nice change from looking a man straight in the eye, or down on him, as was more often the case.

Ben hadn't returned by the time the food was ready and she wondered what on earth was keeping him. The smell of cooking should have brought him back before now. She herself was almost drooling, and yet she couldn't bring herself to begin without him. It wouldn't be proper.

She was fretting about the meal spoiling when he finally appeared, his arms full of branches which he dropped beside the fire. 'You didn't have to do that,' she scolded, because wood-gathering wasn't a proper chore for a man when there was a woman about. 'I've got more than enough for the fire.'

'It's early. We'll keep it going longer tonight.'

'Oh.' Sanna searched his face as she gave him his loaded plate. Camping early, a fire kept going—was it tonight he planned to make her his woman? She could find no answer in his expression.

Had he, like she, merely needed time to get over the feeling of strangeness? It seemed incredible to her, when she reckoned it up, that she had known him for less than forty-eight hours. Such was his impact on her that Vargas and the store could be a million miles away and a hundred years in the past. There was only now for her, and Mr Maddox. Everything that had gone before seemed insignificant.

And she wasn't afraid at all except, perhaps, of not pleasing him. She felt she had sufficient love for both of them, and yet it was so important that she should make him care for her as well. Sharing a blanket might be a permanent bonding for a woman—at least, her kind—

but she knew it was different for a man. Unless he loved her he wouldn't want to keep her, and all her splendid dreams would be shattered.

It was true that she still wanted her fine house and all her pretty things, but Mr Maddox had become an inextricable part of her dream pictures. She would never be able to weave another man into his place, and everything else she craved would become meaningless. She knew that with such chill certainty that she studied his face with fresh anxiety.

There was still sufficient light to see the depthless clarity of his blue eyes as they met her gaze. After a moment he risked a question, hoping it wouldn't release the usual flood of words from her. 'Something on your mind?'

Sanna's usual candour was hindered by a rush of shyness. 'I was wondering . . . camping early, keeping a fire going . . . it doesn't seem like you.'

'Good. I'd hate to be predictable.'

'Oh.' For once she couldn't think of anything else to say.

He finished his food and drank only one cup of coffee before taking his towel and soap and leaving her. Sanna lingered on by the fire, wishing she didn't feel quite so tired. When her chores were done, she told herself, no doubt a good wash would banish her weariness.

The theory seemed all right, but as she skirted the bushes and went among the trees to clean the pans, her lethargy increased. She had to force herself to make her usual thorough job of the washing up, and, when she returned, her feet were dragging. She could scarcely be more tired if she'd walked all day.

A damp towel was spread over the bushes, but no

dirty washing had been left out. 'Mr Maddox!' she called, and waited. There was no answer. With a shrug she went back to the stream and did her own washing, trying to figure out whether he genuinely liked to be independent or whether he was just plain awkward.

It was very private among the trees and the wind had died as suddenly as it had sprung up, encouraging Sanna to strip off and stand in the stream to wash herself. The cold water did not revive her as she'd hoped, and she was yawning as she trudged back to the camp.

The fire had been built up, his blanket was spread out, but of Mr Maddox himself there was no sign. Sanna was exasperated. Her aching muscles yearned for rest, and she knew that the minute she stopped moving she would be asleep. She untied her blanket and looked around. Where was she supposed to put it? Next to his? Or would she wake in the morning to find he'd moved away from her?

It was all too much of a problem for Sanna, whose eyes were closing of their own volition. She had struggled through her chores, she was exhausted, and that was all there was to it. If it was on his mind to make love to her tonight, he should have stayed around. With the best will in the world she could not wait up for him.

She shook out her blanket so that it settled next to his, dropped to her knees and collapsed under it. Tomorrow, she thought vaguely, she would be more accustomed to continuous hours in the saddle, and this dreadful aching would ease. Tomorrow she would be perky enough to stay awake all night if necessary. Tomorrow . . .

Sanna was in a deep and dreamless sleep when something penetrated her unconscious mind and jerked her awake. Her eyes opened. She had no idea how long she had been sleeping or what had disturbed her. She lay unmoving and just managed to make out the blanketed form of Mr Maddox next to her. She could see little else, for the bright moonlight pierced the trees only in patches, and they were lying in shadow.

Her vision wasn't helped by the thick strands of hair lying across her face. She lifted a hand to push them back, frowning as she sought for a reason for waking up in what seemed the middle of the night, when her hand was seized and she was pulled into a sitting position.

She gasped, but the sound was lost when a gun fired so close to her that it seemed to be exploding inside her head. She screamed as the gun fired again and again, and she saw a dim figure aiming at the blanket beside her. Her hair was grasped and her head jerked towards another dim figure crouching over her. She could see the outline of a large hat and bulky shouders, and heard a hoarse chuckle as she began to struggle wildly.

'Mr Maddox! Mr Maddox!' she screamed, although she knew it was useless, for those bullets had been fired at point-blank range.

Her clawing hands dug into pudgy flesh. Vargas, she thought, as she caught the stench of stale sweat, but he cursed her as her nails tore his face, and his voice was different. He twisted his hand cruelly in her hair, bringing stinging tears of pain to her eyes, and forced her back to the ground. 'Hold her, Esteban, while I get my trousers off,' he grunted to his companion. 'She fights like a dozen women.'

'Wait, you fool, while I make sure her man is dead.' The other man reached forward to jerk the blanket away. Sanna tried to turn her head to see, but the grip on her hair was too tight. She moaned in anguish for the man she loved and then jumped involuntarily as there was another explosion. Esteban was lifted off his feet and thrown forward, to lie unmoving.

Shock froze both Sanna and the man she was fighting for a split second, then suddenly she knew that the last shot had been from a rifle, and it could have been fired only by Mr Maddox. She screamed his name and struggled with renewed frenzy. She was struck a vicious blow across her face that all but stunned her, and was pulled to her feet by her hair.

The man was using her as a shield as he turned towards the bushes and fired his pistol into them, then he was retreating, dragging her with him. Sanna went limp and dragged her heels to slow him down, but to little effect, for next she felt the stinging recoil of branches as she was dragged backwards through more bushes. The open circle of the campsite disappeared, and she yelled, 'I'm here, Mr Maddox. I'm here!'

Her assailant's hand found and tightened round her throat, pressing away all sound, and as she choked for air the rifle sounded again, this time from behind her. Suddenly she was face down on the ground, sprawled helplessly beneath the body of the man who had been abducting her. She wriggled ineffectively to free herself, and whimpered when a pair of leather boots came into her line of vision, 'I thought you were under that blanket. I thought . . .'

She gasped with relief as he lifted the body from her and dragged it into a patch of moonlight in the camp. Sanna scrambled to her feet and followed him hastily, scared of the black menace of the bushes now that the peace of the night had been so violently shattered.

Ben was staring dispassionately at the body when she joined him. 'Another of Vargas's enterprising relatives?' he asked.

Sanna glanced at the heavily jowled face with its black moustachios drooping into a thick beard, and shuddered. 'No. I've never seen him before.'

'What about the other one?' He dragged the second body into the moonlight and stood back.

She shook her head. He was much older and slighter, and his lips were drawn back to reveal large protruding teeth in a macabre leer, as though he were sharing one last jest with the devil. 'No. I'd never forget that face. That's not to say they didn't use the store. I told you how Vargas made me hide when bad men came. He'd never have let me cook for you if there'd been somebody else with you.'

Ben picked up the hat that had belonged to the younger, chubby Mexican. It was a sombrero frayed ragged at the brim, but a belt was buckled incongruously around the crown. He tilted the hat so that the buckle gleamed in the moonlight, and wondered if that was what had flashed in the sun and warned him they were being followed after their afternoon rest.

Ben looked at their shoddy clothing and old-fashioned pistols and muskets, thought of the stupidity with which they'd blundered into the trap he'd set for them, and was surprised they'd lived as long as they had. The important thing was that, now he'd had a good look at them, he was sure they had nothing to do with Harry Kirby. He'd never have used such a pair of incompetent bandits. They must have a camp on the mountain somewhere from which they preyed on solitary travellers or groups more poorly equipped than themselves. Such men would kill for a pair of boots—or a belt to decorate a worn-out hat.

Sanna shook his arm. 'Mr Maddox, do you think we could move on? I don't like this place any more.'

Ben heaved the body of the younger bandit over his shoulder. 'There's nothing wrong with the place. We just have to get rid of the uninvited guests.'

He strode off towards the ravine. Sanna ran after him. 'Don't leave me alone! I don't feel safe. That one you've got there was all set to rape me.'

'What did you expect? I told you you'd be better off at the store.' He dropped the body at the edge of the ravine, then rolled it over. There was a splintering of bushes and the rumble of dislodged earth and stones as he started back for the other one.

When the second bandit was disposed of and they were returning to the camp, she persisted, 'Can we move on? There's a good moon. We could lead the horses until we find another place.'

'No. I'm bedding down. You've had three hours' sleep. I've had none.'

'I reckon none is what I'll be getting for the rest of the night!' Sanna picked up her blanket, wrapped it around her, and sat cross-legged in the middle of the camp. 'I'm too scared to risk closing my eyes.'

She glowered at him as he took off his boots and gun-belt, deeply resenting his total lack of sympathy for the shattered state of her nerves. 'What was under your blanket?' she asked suddenly as he picked it up and moved it to another place.

'Branches.'

Sanna digested this, and fell silent as she pieced it together with other bits of information which hadn't seemed significant at the time. The frequency with which he'd glanced back after they'd rested that afternoon. The unexpectedly early halt. The branches he'd brought into the camp. The fire being built up instead of smothered, so that anyone searching for the camp would have no trouble in finding it.

'You were never under that blanket,' she burst out. 'I thought you'd heard them coming and got away in time, but you knew hours ago we were going to be attacked. You set a trap and left me right in the middle of it!'

'You took long enough to work that out,' he replied, holding his blanket up to the moonlight and looking at the bullet-holes in it. Fortunately the bandit hadn't fallen on it, so it was free of bloodstains. It would have been a different story, Ben mused, if he *had* been under it.

'I didn't believe you could be so rotten. I trusted you.'

'More fool you. I told you plain enough yesterday that my skin is more important than yours to me.'

'I would have been on your conscience if I'd been shot.'

'What conscience? You invited yourself along. Perhaps now you'll have the sense to accept that you've a good chance of ending up dead. You can take some supplies and start back to the store tomorrow.' Ben spread out his blanket and put his cocked rifle beside it.

'You'd like that, wouldn't you? Well, I won't go. I'll just watch out more for myself in future. Come to think of it, you probably wanted me shot.'

Ben yawned. 'There wasn't much chance of that. I wanted them so confident they wouldn't be too cautious. I loosened your hair and spread it over the blanket so that they could see right off which one they had to kill.'

'I'm much obliged, I'm sure,' Sanna snapped. 'I didn't know I had you to thank for having my hair half pulled out, my face whacked and very nearly being raped.'

'That was your fault for struggling. If you hadn't, I could have got a clear shot first at the bandit who grabbed you. As it was, I had to risk circling behind him. You damn nearly messed everything up by fighting like that.'

'How thoughtless of me,' she spluttered. 'I just happened to think you were dead and I was on my own. If you'd told me what was going to happen, I'd have known what to do.'

'You wouldn't have slept, and I wanted everything to be nice and natural.'

'You're heartless. You used me as . . . as . . . bait!'

'It's over, and you're all right, so what are you moaning about?'

'I'm scratched and bruised and I've been scared out of my wits. I have a right to moan.'

'You gave up any rights when you forced yourself on me.' He came over and stood in front of her and held out his hand.

'You're taking a risk,' she said, staring at it. 'The way I'm feeling, I might just bite it. What do you want?'

'Your knife. As I said, I don't trust women.'

'The way you are, I'm surprised you trust yourself,' she grumbled, giving the knife to him. Her resentful eyes followed him as he walked away. 'Doesn't it mean anything to you that I've been mauled and all shaken up?'

'As *you* said,' he reminded her, 'all's well that ends well.'

She gasped with outrage, and said between gritted teeth, 'Mr Maddox, you are a bastard!'

'Sanna,' Ben replied, rolling himself into his blanket, 'I'm glad you're beginning to understand me at last.'

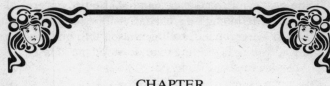

CHAPTER
NINE

SANNA'S REBELLION didn't last long. For one thing she
adored Ben too much to succeed in whipping her resentment into hate. For another, there was something very
soothing about the peaceful way he slept. Such a vigilant
man wouldn't close his eyes for a second if danger still
threatened.

As the frayed edges of her nerves knitted together,
she began to feel ridiculous sitting wrapped in a blanket
in the middle of the camp like a belligerent squaw. And,
as so often happened, something good had come out of
something that was bad. 'Sanna . . .' he had said. She
hadn't liked what he'd said afterwards, but he had finally
used her name!

It had been horrid, being regarded as an anonymous
nuisance. By using her name he had at last acknowledged her as a person. It had been a momentous
moment that she'd been too furious to appreciate at the
time. She appreciated it now, and felt they had crossed
the bridge between being strangers and friends.

What was more, it was perfectly all right for friends to
fall out because they could always make it up again. So
reasoned Sanna, and scolded herself for losing her temper and also for expecting too much from him too soon.
He was a cautious man. That was obvious in every move

he made. It followed that he would be the same in his emotions. Expecting him to fall in love with her right away, as she had fallen for him, was setting her sights too high.

She was the impetuous one. She must learn patience and pin her hopes on worming her way into his affections until he could no longer manage without her.

Sanna, trying to fathom out a man a more experienced woman would have found unfathomable, didn't precisely give up, but she did yawn. The sleep she'd declared wouldn't come to her again that night was overtaking her. She crept over to where he lay, and settled herself down. She was careful not to touch him. She didn't want to wake up to find he had once more moved away from her.

It was Ben who opened his eyes first, conditioned as he was to awake with the dawn. Sanna's face was only inches from his. She looked pale in the grey light, her thick dark eyelashes making pools of shadow against her cheeks, a discoloured patch on her cheekbone bearing witness to her rough treatment by the bandit.

It could have been so much worse, Ben thought, if he hadn't seen that flash of sun on metal the previous afternoon. He looked at her lips. They were parted, temptingly close. He looked a long while, desire raging within him. It would be so easy to reach for her and quench it, but then he thought again how much harder it would be to get rid of her afterwards.

It was her shoulder he finally reached for, and none too gently. 'Time to get up,' he said with all the harshness of a frustrated man.

The rough shaking brought Sanna awake with a start, the fears of the night returning with a rush, but when she saw who it was looking down at her she relaxed. Her mouth curved into a soft smile, almost crumbling Ben's newly stoked up defences.

He turned from her, tossing aside his blanket. Sanna thought wistfully how nice it would be to snuggle cosily down in the cocoon of her blanket until the sun warmed the chill mountain air, but since he showed no more consideration for his own comfort than hers, she could scarcely complain.

She heard him thumping his boots against the ground to dislodge any insects that might have crawled inside during the night, knowing that then he would take his rifle and binoculars to scout the trail ahead.

She smiled secretly to herself as he behaved exactly as she'd predicted. She was getting to know him—and he had called her Sanna! She got up, no longer resisting beginning a new day.

She lit the fire, put water on to heat, and ran to the stream to wash, gingerly splashing water on her sore cheek. She returned to huddle by the fire in her poncho, stretching her cold feet out to the warmth as she swiftly brushed and plaited her hair. She wanted to look nice this morning. She had some apologising to do. That was a nasty name she had called him last night, and now that her rancour had gone she couldn't imagine how she had come to use it.

Sanna was unwrapping the supplies when a gun-shot made her jump out of her skin. She dived for Ben's blanket, found her knife and raced through the trees in the direction he had taken. She saw him coming down a slope before she got far.

'Another bandit?' she cried, flying over the broken ground towards him.

'Breakfast,' he replied, holding a large hare up by its hind legs.

Sanna's alarm vanished in excitement. 'Fresh meat!' she exclaimed, jumping up and down like a two-year-old. 'That's terrific!' She grabbed his arm, squeezed it, took the hare and ran back.

Ben followed more slowly, watching her exuberantly leaping over shrubs, black skirt held high, thick plait bouncing against her back and waving the hare like a trophy. He wondered what she would have done if he'd brought back a deer, which was what he'd hoped for.

She was skinning and gutting the hare by the stream when he caught up with her, looking nothing like the lady she dreamed of being but, under the present circumstances, behaving a great deal more usefully. Ben carried on to set up a spit over the fire so that the meat could be barbecued above the flames.

She was still bouncing with elation when she returned to slide the hare on the spit. She poured water on her hands, dried them, and searched for the salt, saying, 'We could eat what's left at noon, or I could make a stew tonight. What do you think?'

Ben glanced up from the coffee he was stirring into the boiling water. 'I didn't know you were capable of thinking that far ahead.'

'When it comes to food, I'm always thinking.' Sanna added more wood to the outer edges of the fire so that when it had burned through she could push the embers under the meat. The significance of his words sank in. 'You always act as if I'm stupid. Why?'

Ben sipped cautiously from his mug of scalding coffee. 'If you thought there was another bandit, it would have been sensible to run the other way.'

'I thought you might need help.'

He was speechless. He hadn't come across loyalty like that since Gary had been killed, and she owed him no loyalty. He'd suffered some personal anguish to make sure neither of them owed the other anything. He was instantly suspicious, seeing her action as another sign of her determination to cling to him, and answered shortly, 'The day I need help from you, I'd be better off dead.'

'I can understand your not feeling kindly disposed towards me after what I called you last night,' Sanna replied soothingly. 'I don't know how I came to say such a thing, except that when I'm in a temper I can't seem to mind my tongue as I should. I didn't mean it, and I apologise.'

How, Ben fumed, did you snub a woman who had no pride? He said deliberately, 'It was the only sensible thing I've ever heard you say. I may not be a bastard by birth like you, but I am by inclination.'

'You are a mite thoughtless at times,' she conceded. 'But you are not spiteful, so you can't be a—what I called you.'

'I might have known you couldn't keep thinking straight.' Ben leaned forward to turn the hare on the spit. 'It's burning.'

'Hey!' Sanna slapped his hand away. 'It's coming on nicely. Too many cooks spoil the broth, as Mr Blakeney would say.'

He glowered at her. 'To hell with Mr Blakeney and his sayings. We had a better one in the army—God sent meat and the devil sent cooks.'

To his amazement she doubled up with laughter, and the more he glared at her, the more she laughed. 'I'm sorry,' she gasped. 'I haven't heard that one before and it seems so funny coming from you. And here we are, lucky to be alive, and all we can do is squabble how to cook a piece of meat. Doesn't that strike you as ridiculous?'

He was so much taken aback by her laughter that he ignored her question. He was trying to remember whether he had ever been so young and carefree that he could laugh over nothing. Yes, but it seemed a lifetime ago—somebody else's lifetime. He had nothing in common with the youth he had been before the war, and her spontaneous laughter reminded him of how much he had lost of himself—as well as his family.

Her life had been no picnic, either. He wondered how laughter could come so easily to her, but didn't it always, to those who weren't right in the head?

Sanna wiped the tears of mirth from her eyes and asked the question that was making him frown. 'Don't you ever laugh, Mr Maddox?'

He evaded it. 'Burning meat doesn't amuse me.'

She sighed, turned the meat to make him happy, and changed what was obviously a touchy subject. 'You mentioned the army. The first time I saw you I knew you'd been a soldier. It's in the way you stand and walk. Very straight, very proud. I like that. I saw lots of soldiers when the war was starting, all swanky in their grey uniforms. Did you wear a grey uniform?'

He looked away from her, remembering . . . He and his men, towards the end, had worn anything that still had enough thread to hold together. There were as many homespun jackets as grey tunics, cocky feathers stuck into all manner of soft hats, and as often as not rawhide moccasins replacing boots that had fallen apart. It was during the last desperate year of the war that he'd learned to do without sugar. That went only to the hospitals, and they were lucky if they could get meat and bread.

But meagre food and worn-out uniforms aside, his men were superb riders, first-class shots and apparently immune to reverses, for nothing had daunted their jaunty recklessness or their spirit to win. That was why they'd taken the final surrender more as an act of betrayal than one of mercy. It still rankled with Ben, trained not to accept a fight was over until it was won.

'Yes,' he said finally. 'I wore grey.'

Sanna nodded. 'That's the way I figured it. You fought for the South, then, and the South lost. I'm truly sorry about that and I can understand why you're not a happy man, but there's something I'm really desperate to know. Those lovely big houses, Mississippi way—they weren't hurt, were they?'

Ben thought of all the wrecked plantations he had seen. 'A lot of them are nothing but ruins.'

'Oh . . .' Her breath escaped in a disbelieving sigh. 'How could anyone hurt anything so beautiful?'

He didn't answer. Houses could be rebuilt, but the dead couldn't be brought back to life. As usual, she had her priorities wrong.

Sanna, coping with what was, for her, a major catastrophe, scarcely dared ask, 'You said a lot were ruined. Does that mean some aren't hurt at all?'

He nodded, and this time her sigh was one of relief. 'That's all right, then. Mr Blakeney said the war wouldn't do the South any good, which was why he was set on getting away from it. We went down into Texas and then he said the thing to do was get to California. He didn't reckon the war would reach that far. We were on our way when the Apaches got us.'

Ben turned the meat again, and this time Sanna was so preoccupied with her memories that she didn't interfere. Then she asked hesitantly, 'About your house, Mr Maddox. Was that near a battle?'

'No.'

'Where would it be, then?'

'New Mexico.'

'Well, that's right next to Texas. I know, because we had to go through there to get to California, only we didn't get very far. Would your house be big and white with fancy verandas and show grass and trees that don't get chopped down for wood?'

'It's nothing like the plantations you have in mind.'

'Oh.' It was a blow, but Sanna resolutely swallowed it. 'Does it have an upstairs?'

'No.'

'It's not like the store, is it?' she asked in alarm.

'No.'

'Well, then, we can build an upstairs and paint it white. I reckon that will do the trick.' She came down to earth with a thump when she saw his expression. Her tongue had run away with her again. 'I mean we could if you took it in to your head to marry me. I'm not saying you will, mind. Only *if*.'

'There's no *if* about it. I won't. Ever.'

Sanna couldn't see the sense in making him crankier by arguing, not until she was properly his woman, and made another sudden change of subject. 'My, this meat is smelling good. What do you say to slicing off the cooked bits as we want them?'

Ben nodded. She waited politely for him to take the

first slice, then helped herself. He was using his knife and fingers, so she did, too, and neither said any more until they'd had their fill. The hare was a big one, but they were both young and healthy, so there wasn't much left.

'A stew it is tonight, then,' Sanna said, wrapping up the bones. 'I wish I had some onions. Never mind, I'll see what I can do with salt and beans. Who knows, you might be able to shoot something else before sundown.'

'It will be you if you don't stop sucking your fingers like that.'

'Sorry, but you licked yours.'

'I didn't try to swallow them.' Ben stood up and kicked dirt over the fire, the signal that it was time to break camp.

They worked so smoothly together that they were soon on their way, Sanna snug in her poncho, her hat swinging from its strap down her back. Early morning and early evening were the best parts of the day, she mused. It was getting through the hours between that was the struggle.

They left the ravine behind and, although their pace was steady, it was also slow. They appeared to be going down as many slopes as up, but in fact they were climbing all the time, which was tiring for the horses. The sun made them sweat, flies pestered. Sanna retreated behind her hat and veil.

The hours passed and their eyes became fixed on a burst of green on the mountain, as tempting as an oasis in a desert. When they got nearer they were able to identify willows and cottonwoods with healthy water-nourished leaves.

Sanna gave a whoop of glee and cantered ahead with the pack-horse, while Ben approached more warily. In the centre of the trees was a pool made by a stream spilling from the top of the mountain, then widening and slowing. She slipped from her saddle, threw off her hat and splashed cool water over her hot face. Then she and the horses drank.

Ben came to the pool and dismounted, and while he and his horse drank, she lifted her skirts and paddled. When he had finished she jumped up and down, laughing as the water splashed her legs and clothes. 'It's not deep enough to swim, but we can soak and float,' she cried excitedly.

There was no answer, and when she looked round she saw Ben climbing back into his saddle. 'Aren't we stopping here?' she asked, her expression so crestfallen it was almost ludicrous. 'It's about noon, and we'll never find a better place to rest.'

'No.'

'Why? I'm hot and dusty. I want to bathe and . . . and have fun!'

Ben took the leading rein of the pack-horse and rode past her. 'Suit yourself. I'm not here to play games.'

Sanna stamped her foot, her fists clenching. 'You're the most selfish man I've ever come across. You're not human! It's not natural to ride past a place like this after the hours we've been sweating in the saddle. Do you hear me? It's not natural!'

For all the attention he paid her she might have been whispering instead of shouting. She swore fluently in Spanish, scrambled on to Magpie and cantered after him.

When she caught up, she plonked her veiled hat on her head and glared at him. 'Why do you have to be such a killjoy? That place was beautiful. What's more, it had good water, good shade and sweet grass for the horses. It makes sense to stop there. Isn't that what you're always on about—sense!'

'You never learn, do you, Sanna? In spite of the Indians and the bandits, you're still assuming we've got the mountain to ourselves. Those trees mean water. They can be seen for miles, an attraction, for sure. It's the worst place to stop, unless you happen to enjoy bad company.'

'Oh.' Sanna thought about that, then said grumpily, 'Why didn't you explain? Why let me get mad?'

'I don't know why I'm bothering now. You're still moaning.'

'Well . . . well . . .' she spluttered. 'I thought I had something to moan about.' She glanced at him and succumbed once more to the powerful attraction he had for her. And, as usual, her resistance crumbled. 'Seems I owe you another apology. I'll tell you something, though. I know why you bothered to explain. It's because you're not as bad as you make out.'

'No,' he agreed, wishing she'd stop seeing good where there was none. 'I'm worse.'

'I don't believe that. I think something bad happened to you the way something bad happened to me. I went funny after the Indians captured me. I hated everything and everybody. It didn't last, though. Nobody can go on hating for ever.'

'I can.'

'You'll stop when something good happens for you,' Sanna predicted confidently. Privately she saw herself as that 'something good'. She would love away all his bitterness just as soon as he would let her. Thinking about it, she was swamped by the yearning to teach him that, although life might be one long battle against adversity, the good bits in between were there to be seized and enjoyed.

They were riding at the base of a sheer mass of rock with cliff-like sides. This time they heard the water before they saw it, for over millions of years the waterfall had worn a deep recess in the rock. At its base was a pool partially shaded by the cliff. The earth above the rock was too shallow to support trees, but there were plenty of shrubs and grass. If the pool they had recently passed seemed like an oasis, this was a paradise for hot and grimy travellers.

'It's beautiful,' Sanna gasped. 'Oh, Mr Maddox, can we stop this time?'

Ben looked around. The cliff was at their backs and there was a good view for miles below them. For answer he dismounted and unsaddled his horse. He left it to graze while he stripped off his clothes.

Sanna was hopping with excitement as she unsaddled Magpie and took the pack from the other horse. She heard a splash, and when she looked round he was already in the pool.

She was running to the edge to join him when he rose, flicked water from his hair and turned on his back to float. She stopped abruptly. He hadn't a stitch on.

Sanna stared, realised what she was doing, and abruptly turned her back on him. She was prepared to discard her skirt—but to plunge in *naked*! She couldn't do that. Nor, when she thought it over, would he expect her to. What he would be expecting was for her to keep out of the way while he bathed first. What if he'd seen her gawking at him? She blushed right down to her shoulders and sat down with her back to the pool.

She tried very hard to be patient, but she literally itched to get into the water. She would be able to wash her hair, too. She unpacked the towel and soap and risked a look round. He was climbing out of the pool and stretching himself on a rock in the sun as shamelessly as though she weren't there at all.

Sanna grabbed her hairbrush and the towel and soap and, with eyes averted, walked to the pool. She slipped out of her skirt and plunged in, the cool water enfolding her hot and itchy body like a benison. She swam in and out of the waterfall, gasping, laughing, submerging, floating and splashing in an ecstasy of delight.

Ben heard her cavorting in the water, and pretty soon he was watching her. It was impossible not to. The white cotton of her blouse and trousers clung to her, revealing rather than concealing the pinky-white glow of her skin. She turned on her back and kicked her way to the edge of the pool, the sun catching droplets of spray and turning them briefly into diamonds before they fell back into the pool.

She began soaping her head and, when she sank under the water to rinse it, her fair hair spread across the surface of the pool, the lather floating away. Ben wanted to dive in and clasp her gleaming body against his. *No*, said his brain. *Yes*, craved his aching body.

Abruptly he stood up, pulled on his trousers and strode to the supplies. The unreasoning anger he always felt when she tempted him beyond endurance was very close to hate as he sat with his back to her and began to chew some dried meat savagely.

When Sanna climbed from the pool, she saw he was being as discreet as she had been, and went to the rock where he had dried himself. She stripped off her trousers and blouse, wrapped herself in the towel, and lay face down so that the sun could dry her hair without freckling her complexion.

She moved layers of her hair this way and that until it was no more than slightly damp, then sat up to brush it. She was shaking it back from her face so that it fell in a gleaming mass over her shoulders, when Ben looked round.

He had to. He was not, as she had stated such a short time ago, inhuman. He had fought a long hard battle against temptation. When he saw her beside the pool, her curves inadequately wrapped in a towel and with the sun turning her fair hair to molten gold, he knew the battle was lost.

The first Sanna knew that he was beside her was when he touched her hair, his hand sliding down its silken strands. She sat quite still. His hand left her hair and strayed to her bare shoulder, tentatively, as if giving either of them a chance to pull back.

Sanna felt no fear. This is the way it should be, she thought. This is right. She bent her head and rubbed her cheek lovingly against his hand, and instantly his grasp changed from tentative to assured.

CHAPTER
TEN

A DELICIOUS THRILL quivered through Sanna as she felt
the power come into Ben's fingers. She had wanted so
many things. A silk cushion, a silk dress, a white house.
Now only his touch was important. Everything else was
suddenly superficial.

She raised her head and looked at him, a dreamy soft
glow in her eyes, her lips parted in wonder. She wasn't
sure how to express the love burning within her, so she
placed her cheek against his and nuzzled him gently,
glorying in the roughness of his growing beard against
her tender skin. She drew away slightly, looking at his
firm lips and longing to press hers against them, but
lacking the courage. And so she contented herself with
lifting her fingers to trace the outline of his mouth while
she waited for him to kiss her.

Ben frowned slightly, unprepared for such innocent
overtures. He had expected the unmistakably direct
response of an experienced woman, yet she was behaving like a girl alone with her sweetheart for the first time.
He could see no guile in her deep blue eyes nor feel any
provocative movement of her body against his.

He didn't know whether she was trying to tease him or
dupe him by feigning innocence, but he was in no mood
to play games. He coiled his hands in her silky hair and

held her head steady while he kissed her with a passion that had been leashed too long.

A sensation so sweet that it bordered on anguish shot through Sanna, making her gasp and clutch at him as if she would have collapsed without his support. His second kiss was even more demanding in its intensity, exploding through her nervous system and making her lose what little grasp she still had on reality.

She was scarcely aware of Ben sweeping her up in his arms and carrying her to a shady place on the grass, for he was still kissing her, causing wave after wave of pleasure to tingle through her until they overlapped and her whole body was awash with desire.

She murmured incoherent words of love, and clung to him. This, she thought deliriously, was loving. This was belonging .

Ben's lips moved from her mouth to her throat and along her shoulder, his own senses swimming as he pulled the towel from her body and kissed her breasts. He unbuckled his belt and kicked off his trousers, still kissing her, and then he was exploring her unresisting thighs.

There was an unbelievable joy in looking at and touching the perfection of her body, but he could no longer hold himself in check. She must have sensed it, for he heard her say, 'I don't know about this . . . you'll have to teach me . . .' The words scarcely penetrated his brain. The throbbing of his body was too intense for him to consider anything but its appeasement.

He moved on top of her, felt her arms tighten around him, and by the time he discovered she was telling the truth it was too late. Her teeth bit savagely into his shoulder, goading him on, and they were one.

For Sanna it was a total consummation, involving her
heart, her body and her soul. She learned how close
ecstasy and agony could be, and how sublime the subsequent satisfaction, how deep the peace.

For Ben it was the slaking of a lust which had become
unendurable, with the added triumph of knowing that he
had made her want him as much as he wanted her. He
might have unwittingly taken her innocence, but their
pleasure had been mutual, which exonerated him from
any obligation towards her.

Not that he thought of any of this until after they had
fallen asleep in each other's arms and he awakened to
find his head cradled against her breast. What re-kindled
his hostility towards her was the swift discovery that the
satisfaction of making love to her had been only fleeting.
He was not at peace with himself. He wanted her again.

Ben was furious at his own weakness, and at her
ability to make him forget everything but the seductive
delights of her body. He eased himself away from her.
He had to conquer the urge to kiss and caress her once
more into passion. If she awoke before he had the battle
won, she would discover the power she had over him and
trade on it, as women always did.

He dragged his eyes from the provocative curves of
her breasts and hips and looked up at the sun. It was
waning. He stood up, his fury increasing. They had
slept away good riding hours. She was slowing him
down, side-tracking him from his task with her cursed
sensuality.

Ben glanced down at her, this time coldly. He knew he
wouldn't be able to stay away from her, not now, but he
could ration himself. It would take a lot of willpower. He
didn't begrudge that, not when the reward was regaining

total control over his actions. The problem would re-solve itself, of course, as soon as he found somebody to take her off his hands.

He looked down at his own body. He was his own man again. His brain had overcome his physical weakness. He was able to walk away from her, push her out of his mind, wash and dress and leave her to see whether anything was moving on the mountain since he'd last looked.

Sanna awoke suffering none of the soul-searchings that had bedevilled Ben. She would have loved to find him beside her, but she felt none of her usual apprehension when he was missing. She was his now, which meant he was also hers. He would be back.

She stretched languorously, the euphoric afterglow of his lovemaking undimmed by her deep sleep. She yawned, blinked lazily at the sun and realised from its position that they must be staying for the night. There could be only one explanation. Her beloved Mr Maddox was as reluctant as herself to leave this beautiful place where they had found such happiness.

Sanna smiled, remembering how deep and savage had been his need for her, glorying in it but feeling humble, too, because she loved him so. She wanted to stay where she was, re-living every precious moment, and yet the stronger need to be fresh and beautiful for him when he returned brought her to her feet.

She bathed and dressed and brushed her hair. She touched her lips, which still felt crushed from his de-manding kisses, and then she remembered the bruise on her cheek, worrying in case it marred her beauty. She wanted so much to be perfect for him.

Sanna recalled that his beard had been no more than

stubble when she'd first seen him, and wondered if he had a shaving-mirror in his saddle-bags. She went to them, opened one and reached inside. She pulled out a soft leather pouch which looked a good place to keep a mirror. She loosened the draw-string and blinked as jewellery tumbled into her lap, gold and precious stones gleaming against the black cotton of her skirt.

She picked up a ring, her lips forming a soundless 'Oh!' of wonder at the sapphire which was as blue as her eyes. Then there was a painful grip on her wrist and the ring fell back into her lap.

'You don't have to steal,' Ben told her grimly. 'You'll get paid.'

Sanna twisted her head to stare up at him. There was none of the love she had expected to see on his face, only harshness and contempt. 'I . . . I wasn't stealing,' she stammered, totally bewildered that he could behave like this after what had happened between them.

'And I wasn't born yesterday.' Ben released her, scooped the jewellery from her skirt back into the pouch and strapped it into his saddle-bag.

Her bewilderment increased. 'Why should I get paid?'

'For services rendered.' When he saw the puzzled frown between her eyebrows, he said more explicitly, 'For sleeping with me. Whoring.'

Sanna's cheeks whitened and her throat tightened with shock. 'That's a terrible thing to say. You're the first man I ever . . .'

'I know that,' he broke in, 'but it was just a matter of who started you off. Just because it was me doesn't change anything between us.'

'Everything's changed,' she protested disbelievingly. 'I'm your woman now.'

'For the time being. Then you'll be somebody else's. That's the way it goes with women like you.'

Fury flowed through Sanna like a living flame. She leapt to her feet, her fists clenched, her eyes blazing. 'First I'm a thief and then I'm a whore. I should hate you, Mr Maddox. You don't deserve to be loved!'

'That's the truth,' he agreed coldly and moved away from her to begin saddling up his horse.

Sanna ran to her bundle of possessions, snatched up the pouch which contained her own treasures, and ran after him. 'I don't need to steal from you! I've got my own pretty things. Look!'

She tipped the contents of the pouch on to a rock and grasped him by the shoulder to pull him round. Ben glanced down. Among the small stones she had found and kept over the years for the beauty of their colours were a wire brooch with beads strung on it, which had a broken pin; an ornamental Spanish hair-comb with several of the tortoiseshell teeth missing; a leather book-mark bearing remnants of gold lettering; a metal buckle with paste stones; a faded blue velvet ribbon; a tarnished pair of nail-scissors with both ends snapped off; a small piece of Indian beadwork and a collection of unmatched silver buttons.

Ben was about to say he had never seen a bigger collection of rubbish in his life, when she went on triumphantly, 'So you see, I don't need to steal! I was only looking for a mirror so that I would know what this bruise on my face looks like. Why, when I'm cooking, I don't even steal bits of food when you're not around to watch. Do you still think I'm a thief?'

Ben turned back to his horse, tightening the cinches. 'If it will shut you up, no.'

'What about a whore?' she challenged.

'Maybe you'll get lucky and somebody will marry you. Only don't expect it to be me.' Ben moved on to get the pack-horse ready.

Sanna scooped her treasures into the pouch and followed him. 'Why not me? We're right together. You know we are. Like one person.'

'Any woman's right when a man wants one,' he told her dispassionately.

Sanna stamped her foot, making his horses fidget nervously. 'That's not true! You keep spoiling everything by saying nasty hurtful things. I'm not *any* woman. I'm *your* woman.'

'No, you're not. I've already got one.'

'You're married?' Shock made her voice rise to a screech. In her dreams, the man she picked might have been a shadowy figure, but he had never been married. The possibility just hadn't occurred to her.

Ben glanced warily at her, climbed into his saddle and reached for the pack-horse's rein. If she was going to become hysterical, he wasn't leaving one of his animals in her care.

'I said, are you married?' Sanna shouted as he began to turn his horses round her.

'I shall be. She's waiting.'

That wasn't so bad. Relief had scarcely calmed Sanna's panic before she was demanding, 'Is she as beautiful as I am?'

'She's different.'

'What do you mean, different?'

'She's a lady.' Ben touched his heels to his horse's sides and left her standing in a swirl of dust.

'Let's see how much of a lady she is when she finds out

about me,' she yelled after him. 'Because I swear to you, Mr Maddox, that I'm the one you're going to marry. So there!' She stamped her foot again, began to choke on the dust and stalked her way out of it.

Grimly she gathered her belongings and saddled up Magpie. Her hands were shaking with temper, but beneath it was a great suffocating lump of sadness. Why did nothing ever go right for her? She tried and tried, but her chasing happiness was like trying to dig a gopher out of the ground. Every time she thought she had it trapped, it escaped through another hole.

Another woman, indeed! All the hate she should be feeling for him, only she couldn't, she directed towards her faceless enemy. She hated her so hard it soothed her temper and deflected her anger away from the man who had done his level best to deserve it.

By the time she mounted Magpie she had muttered and cursed her way into a more philosophic frame of mind. The other woman—the lady, no less!—might have the advantage of silks and curls, but if she were hundreds, maybe thousands, of miles away, what good could they do her?

Sanna, whose geography was so hazy it was more of a fog, and who had no idea how long a mile was, measured distances more conveniently in the time it took to cover them. Sitting motionless in the saddle and pondering deeply, she came to the comforting conclusion that she had weeks in which to prove to Mr Maddox she was all he wanted in a woman, and more. The lady part she could learn as she went. She'd already improved her eating so much that he no longer complained.

In fact, she decided, the one really in need of re-educating was Mr Maddox himself. He didn't know when he was happy, and that was a terrible thing. It would be a joy to teach him, only she'd have to be cunning, of course. He seemed very set in his ways and might not take kindly to being eased into new ones.

A lizard scuttled in front of Magpie, bringing Sanna out of her reverie and making her realise the man she was weaving her plots around was getting farther away by the minute. Even so, she didn't immediately gallop after him. She walked her horse across the camp, staring at the waterfall and the pool to fix it in her mind for ever.

This was the place she would think of on bad days when she needed something good to hold on to. Here Mr Maddox had been all hers for a little while, whatever he had said afterwards. They had been two people, blissfully, totally one. Sanna rode away knowing that she wouldn't swop places with the distant, waiting lady for all the silks in the world.

She was singing when she caught up with Ben, making him think once more that she wasn't quite right in the head. He had been expecting the verbal battle to be resumed, but she smiled at him like a woman without a grudge or even a single bitter thought.

He was suspicious rather than relieved, trying to anticipate when the next attack would come. When none did, he was puzzled, and that wasn't all he was puzzled about. He asked, 'How is it you were still a virgin?'

'I told you. I didn't grow up until I was with Vargas. I was intended for his son, Eduardo, when he came home from fighting with Juárez. That's why I was in such a panic to get away.'

'Vargas didn't strike me as a man who could keep his hands to himself.'

'I could run rings round him. Whenever he did manage to creep up on me I used to yell for his wife. She used to give him hell. He was dead scared of crossing her, because she kept him safe from her Apache relations.' Sanna paused, then added with a chuckle, 'I'm pretty good at yelling.'

'You don't have to tell me,' he replied feelingly.

'I'll sing to you if you prefer,' she offered with a wicked sideways look at him.

It sounded suspiciously as if she were teasing him. He looked sharply at her and, instead of answering, asked what was on his mind. 'If you had no experience, where did you get the nerve to offer yourself to me at the store?'

'Oh, I didn't need any nerve when you were a stranger. I needed it after I knew you, crosspatch that you are,' she replied sweetly. There was a stunned silence, and she burst into laughter. 'You should see your face! Hasn't anybody ever joked with you before? No wonder you're always so serious.'

'It's one up on being an idiot,' he growled.

'At least I'm a happy one—mostly, which is more than I can say for you. One of these days you're going to smile and I'm going to faint right off my horse with shock.' Getting no encouragement from him, she sighed. 'All right, I'll be serious. If you really want to know, I was so set on getting away from the store I didn't get scared until we were bedding down that first night. I was scared silly then, only it didn't last. It couldn't, with me loving you so.'

'Stop saying that,' he snapped. 'How old are you?'

'I don't know.'

'Everybody knows how old they are.'

'Only if they have somebody to tell them. Mr

Blakeney said I was three when he bought me, but he would never tell me how many years I'd been with him. He wanted me to stay a little girl. He said years didn't matter, only getting too big did.'

'When did the Indians get you?'

'A few months, maybe a year, after your war started. I was with them three winters. I reckon time that way because Mr Blakeney said anybody with the sense to tell one season from another didn't need calendars. I missed being a squaw by the skin of my teeth, because right after I was sold to Vargas, I became a woman.'

Sanna shuddered. 'Do you know some squaws have blue tattoos on their faces? I was terrified that would happen to me. When you come to think of it, I've been as lucky as I've been unlucky.'

She got no response because Ben was working out how old she was. Given the variable age at which a girl reached puberty, he placed her somewhere between fifteen and seventeen—the age at which he'd run away to war. Well, he'd still had a lot to learn then, and so, it seemed, had she.

He was mystified by the way she could bounce back laughing after the bitter scenes they'd had, but he was also reassured. She was resilient. She would take up easily enough with another man when the time came. She must be one of those shallow females whose emotions never ran deep enough to be troublesome.

Sanna took his long silence to mean that he had once more withdrawn from her. To entertain herself, she began to sing.

'Shut up,' Ben ordered.

'I love you, too,' Sanna said, and giggled.

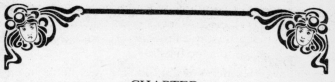

CHAPTER
ELEVEN

THERE HAD been many strange episodes in Sanna's life but none so bizarre as her relationship with Ben over the following days. Although during the daylight hours his attitude to her was unchanged, at night he reached for her with a passion that belied his indifference.

She stoically endured the snubs and hardships of the day, living for the nights when he had a need for her. She yearned for words of love he never spoke, remaining cheerfully confident that they would come.

He still took her knife at night and she would try not to giggle, for he didn't share her sense of the ridiculous. Sometimes she ached as much to hear him laugh as she ached for him to put his feelings into words. When the mood took her she teased him mercilessly, refusing to be cowed. She had learned that, for all his scowls and scathing remarks, he was never brutal. According to her standards, based as they were on rough usage, that made him a good man and, all in all, she was blissfully happy.

Ben was aware of it and was baffled. He thought that if she could be happy with him she could be happy with anybody, and her constant talk of love was just so much foolishness.

One night they lingered longer than usual round the fire, wrapped in blankets against the keen wind, sleepily content after feasting on the remains of a young deer Ben had shot two days before. They were lulled by the sound of a creek near by and the swaying branches of fragrant pines.

Ben was bearded now and looked very fierce in the glow from the dying fire, but Sanna sensed his mellowness. It gave her the nerve to ask one of the questions he never encouraged. 'Mr Maddox, where exactly are we going?'

'The village of San Mari-Luz.'

'Where's that?'

'Somewhere in these mountains.'

She was none the wiser, but she persisted, 'Is that where you'll find the man you are after?'

Ben nodded.

'What's his name?'

'Kirby.'

'What did he do that was so terrible you followed him all this way?'

'He led a band of *comancheros* on an attack of my home. The house held out, but he caught my father, brother, sister and stepmother in the open. He killed my brother and stepmother, carried off my sister and left my father to die of his wounds.'

It was the bare bones of the story, but Sanna had enough experience of violence not to need it fleshed out. 'You weren't there?'

'No.'

'And your sister?' Sanna whispered.

'She's dead.'

'I'm sorry.'

'You don't need to be. It's none of your business.'

His mood was veering, but there was still so much she

wanted to know that she asked, 'Are you the last of your family?'

'My father was alive when I took off after Kirby. He was very sick. He's probably dead now.'

'Oh.'

'Yes, "Oh",' Ben mimicked savagely. He was angry that she'd caught him off guard and got the story out of him. Hadn't he said at the beginning that she knew as much about him as she was ever going to? He'd made a liar of himself, and he was damned if he wanted anybody's pity.

Furious, he left the fire and settled down for the night. His resentment towards her was so strong that he would have repulsed her if she'd tried to cajole him.

But Sanna had grown wiser. She sat on by the fire, thinking over what he had told her. She'd never had a family to lose, but she could imagine what it was like. It had been bad enough losing Mr Blakeney, and he had never been an affectionate man.

When she judged enough time had passed, she doused the fire and went to spread her blanket next to Ben's. She lay quietly beside him, letting the warmth and closeness of her body soften him in a way no words could.

They lay side by side, silently locked in a battle of wills. 'Damn you, you witch,' Ben muttered at last, and turned towards her.

Sanna smiled secretively into the darkness as his arms came round her. She had her little triumphs.

At about eleven the next morning the mountain provided them with one of its sudden contrasts. They found themselves looking down on a grassy valley with what appeared to be two villages within an hour's riding of each other.

Ben studied them through his binoculars. One was no village, but a *hacienda* pretty much like his own home. It was built around a series of patios with no windows in the thick outer walls, so that it would be safer against attack. It was a single-storeyed, flat-topped fortress set among neat cultivated fields of vegetables and grain which were irrigated by canals leading from a creek running through the valley.

An army of white-clothed labourers were at work in the fields, and beyond them livestock grazed on rich green grass. A wave of nostalgia swept over Ben, so unexpectedly fierce that it ached like the rawness of an unhealed wound. Perversely, he felt bitter animosity towards Sanna. Her sexuality was insidious, softening his protective shell and making him vulnerable to emotions he could survive more efficiently without.

He swung his glasses along the well-defined track beside the creek leading to the village, which had a church dominating one side of the usual square, and flat-topped houses like so many square boxes along the others. Two roads bisected the village like a cross, leading to nowhere except neat orchards and tidy fields.

Sanna was fidgeting in her saddle, and her excitement bubbled over as she exclaimed, 'Days of nothing and then two villages! Would you ever credit it? Which one are we going to visit?'

Ben nodded to the *hacienda*. 'That's not a village, it's a private estate. What we call a ranch.'

'Truly?' She was incredulous. 'It's as big as a village.

Imagine one family owning all that. Can I borrow your glasses?'

He passed them to her and she studied the *hacienda*, gasping with awe when she saw clearly the beautifully carved main doors with elaborate iron locks, the patios filled with flowers and fruit trees and, in one of them, a fountain sparkling like splintered crystals in the sunshine.

'Water that plays,' she breathed. 'Oh, Mr Maddox, that is . . . is rich! I didn't know a house with no upstairs could be so splendid. I'd feel more than a lady living there, I'd feel a princess.' She broke off to look at him entreatingly. 'Could we visit?'

'I'm not here to make social calls.'

'I thought you'd say something like that.' Sanna sighed, and added regretfully, 'I'd have loved to see inside. When I was with Mr Blakeney we'd visit all the grand houses. Sometimes we were invited into the kitchen for a meal. Maybe you won't believe this, but I've seen kitchens bigger than the whole of Vargas's store—and so clean and fine you'd think the family worked in them instead of the servants.'

She turned her horse to follow Ben as he rode towards the track leading to the village, marvelling, 'I can't get over that place. I thought everything in Mexico was small and mean and dirty. I didn't know there were beautiful places like that.'

She twisted to look once more at the *hacienda*, but it was hidden by a slope. Her expression changed as a very different thought chased from her mind the vision of peace and prosperity the lovely ranch represented. 'Mr Maddox, what if this village is San Mari-Luz?'

Ben thought it looked too open, too prosperous and

too accessible to be chosen as a shelter by Harry Kirby,
but he said, 'I hope it is.'

Sanna put back her veil, her face paler than usual as
she whispered, 'I'm afraid.'

'If Kirby's there, you have reason to be.' Ben looked
towards a clump of trees where the discordant sound of
clanking bells heralded the arrival of a flock of goats.
The lead goat appeared followed by many more, each
with a bell suspended from its neck. 'Wait here,' he said,
and rode towards the boy herding them.

Sanna watched him go, her face strained. She was so
afraid Kirby would kill her Mr Maddox that she felt
physically sick. She chewed her lip while he talked to the
boy, flicked him a coin and rode back.

'It's not San Mari-Luz,' he said, and she couldn't
understand his disappointment, but he didn't explain
how he had felt when he'd learned there were still three
days' hard riding separating him from Kirby.

Dumbly Sanna handed him the leading rein of the
pack-horse, dismounted and was very sick. She washed
her face in the river, clamped on her hat but kept the veil
back for air, and remounted.

'I'm sorry about that, but I was so scared of you
meeting Kirby that it made me ill. I'm better now.'

Ben stared at her, alarmed not by her pallor but by the
possibility she might actually care for him. She'd said she
did often enough, but he'd dismissed that as the need
women had to clothe sex in the wrappings of love. 'You
mean you're scared Kirby will get his hands on you?'

'If he kills you, I won't care what happens to me,' she
replied bleakly. 'Couldn't you just forget him and go
home?'

'No.' Ben rode on, reassured. Womanlike, she was

trying to deflect him from his purpose to carry out her own, which was to get safely over the border. That was self-interest, not love.

Sanna, whose spirits could never stay depressed for long, suddenly said, 'A man like Kirby must have loads of enemies. Maybe somebody else has killed him by now. As Mr Blakeney would say, there's no sense in worrying over something that might never happen.' They had reached the outskirts of the village, and she asked, 'Why are there so many people? What's going on?'

He didn't have to answer, for they had reached the square, and she whooped, 'Market day!' Her eyes sparkled as she saw the variety of goods set out on coloured blankets. There were huge pumpkins, squashes, melons and strings of red and green chillies as bright as beads. One blanket was piled high with woven baskets, while others displayed pottery, tin pots, herbs, jewellery, tiled trays, wood carvings, sombreros, paper flowers and flower-scented soaps.

There was a fiesta air about the people laughing and chattering and bargaining which readily infected Sanna. She smiled at the people who stared curiously at them as they rode slowly through the crowd, her smile only slipping when Ben showed no sign of stopping.

She grabbed his arm. 'We can get all the supplies we need right here.'

'I don't care for haggling. I'll get what's needed at the store.'

'Where's the joy in spending money if you can't save some?' she demanded, yearning to be one of the cheerful bustling throng, but Ben had seen a mass of animal entrails on sale, thick with flies and smelling to high heaven. His nose wrinkled with disgust and he rode on.

Sanna reacted like a child robbed of a treat. 'Give me the money and I'll do the haggling. I'll enjoy it. Why do I have to be miserable just because you are?'

She was speaking to thin air, for he had ridden along the road. She rode sulkily after him, scarcely conscious of the interest she was arousing, although Ben was. He looked at her as they dismounted outside a store, and wasn't surprised. She was scarcely decent. It was obvious there was nothing under the white blouse but Sanna, and her skirt was inches too short, revealing bare ankles and feet.

Aware of his scrutiny, she took off her hat and scowled, unwilling to forgive him yet. A man standing outside the store moved aside as Ben went in, his eyes riveted on Sanna.

He was in his mid-thirties, tall, slim and superbly dressed in the style of a *hidalgo*, a Spanish landowner. His narrow black trousers were embroidered with silver thread at the seams, his white shirt was spotless and his short black jacket fitted his shoulders like a second skin. Silver spurs were attached to his leather boots, and under his flat-topped, flat-brimmed hat his black hair was flecked with grey at the temples.

He surprised Sanna by bowing deeply to her and she gave him a suspicious nod as she followed Ben. In a sunnier mood she would have thought the store a palace in comparison with Vargas's, but she wasn't prepared to see good in anything but the market. The floor and walls were tiled, shelves were piled high with fabrics, blankets and leather goods, and barrels of beans and grain fronted the long counter.

The patron came forward to meet them, smiling and

bowing, his round face topped by a mass of black curls and his breath whistling through a gap in his front teeth as he welcomed them profusely.

Sanna flounced over to a humped chest and sat down, staring sulkily at her feet, while Ben said, 'I have three horses outside that need food and shade.'

'It will be seen to immediately, señor.' The patron turned his head to the curtained alcove at the back of the store, and called, 'Juan!'

A young boy, a miniature of himself but with a perfect white-toothed smile, came running, listened to a string of orders and ran out of the front of the shop to obey them.

Ben ordered his supplies, and then indicated Sanna. 'She needs clothes. What have you got?'

Sanna sat up straight, saying haughtily, 'In silk. I'm not interested in anything else.'

The patron came towards her. 'If it pleases the lady to move, I believe we might find what is needed in this chest.'

Sanna stood up and, when the lid of the chest was raised, her sulks vanished. Among the jumble of clothes inside was a gleam of yellow silk. She seized it and pulled out a dress, her expression changing to dismay when she saw it was ripped and bloodstained across the bodice. 'I don't think the lady who wore this wanted to part with it,' she said.

She looked at Ben and saw from his expression that he was as aware as she of what was in the chest. Loot. She shrugged. 'It's an ill wind . . .' she murmured, and took out a blue silk dress.

The patron explained fearfully, 'Many men who come here for supplies pay in goods, not money. It is wiser not to argue with them. I can only give them what they want and take what they offer. I am a family man, you understand, bred to shopkeeping and not to fighting.'

He looked relieved when Ben offered no comment but merely asked, 'Where can we get some decent food?'

'Just a few paces along the street, señor. My cousin's *cantina*.'

Ben walked to the door, and Sanna emerged from her rummaging in the chest to ask, 'Don't you want to see what I'm choosing?'

'No. Get what you need, but no more than your horse can carry.' He looked at the patron. 'I'll pay when I come back for the supplies.'

Ben walked along the street and into the *cantina*, which was coolly tiled like the store. There was only one other customer, the man dressed in *hidalgo* fashion, who was standing at the bar. Ben sat down, his eyes narrowing as the man came up to him and bowed courteously. 'Permit me to introduce myself, señor. I am Luis Montalban from the *hacienda* which you doubtless passed on your way here. You will honour me by drinking with me?'

Ben nodded and studied Montalban as he sat opposite. He was tall and distinguished-looking, but he lacked the aristocratic features and arrogance of a true *hacendado*, an estate-owner. Probably a bastard son, Ben decided, acknowledged to the point of being given a position of prestige. He wondered what he wanted.

Montalban clicked his fingers and the patron came hurrying with a tray bearing a bottle of tequila, two glasses and a dish of salt. He poured the drinks, bowed, and left them.

Both men put salt on the back of their hands, licked it and tossed the tequila down their throats. There was silence as they resumed their scrutiny of each other, then Montalban began cautiously, 'The matter I wish to discuss with you is delicate, señor, so delicate that I am at a loss how best to broach it. However, a man who does not speak when the time is right must often stay silent for ever, and spend the rest of his life regretting his timidity. You would agree, señor?'

Ben nodded, expressionless, waiting for him to get to the point.

Montalban refilled the glasses. 'I have seen many beautiful women, but never one as lovely as the lady who travels with you. She is your wife?'

'No.' Ben relaxed. Now he knew what the man was after.

'Ah . . . She is your woman, then?'

Ben clicked his fingers, and when the patron came he ordered food for himself and Sanna. Then he replied bluntly, 'She's her own woman. She's travelling with me only until I can find somewhere safe to leave her.'

Montalban's eyes widened and he said swiftly, 'I could offer her such a place. I manage the *hacienda* for the owners, who are away most of the year. It is a position of power and prestige. The lady could have anything she desired.'

'Would you marry her?'

'I would not feel such a beauty was safely mine until she was my wife,' Montalban replied fervently. 'What is your price, señor?'

Ben's eyes hardened. 'I'm not in the slave trade. Ask her. To live in the *hacienda* might be enough.' *With a silk cushion thrown in*, he found himself thinking against his will. She should have her silk dresses by now. She was taking enough time.

He drank his tequila, covered the glass with his hand when Montalban would have refilled it, and called over the patron to order his food to be served and Sanna's to be kept hot.

The patron bowed and hurried into the back room. Montalban refilled his own glass and said, 'I cannot quite believe you are willing to give away such a treasure.'

'Let's say I have another treasure at home.'

'Ah . . . Now I understand. She knows this?' When Ben nodded, he went on, 'Then she will be willing to stay with me?'

'She would if she had any sense, but she hasn't. You'll have to persuade her. It shouldn't be difficult. She's had a rough time with me. Soft words and a few luxuries should do it.'

Montalban inclined his head. 'I know how to treat a woman.'

'I'm sure you do.' Ben leaned back as a black-clothed woman approached with a laden tray and put a variety of dishes in front of him. 'She's got a notion she's fond of me, but it's only because she doesn't know any better. I'll leave her here. From then on it's up to you.'

'Her name?'

'Sanna. She likes to be called Susanna.' Ben picked up his fork and began to eat.

'Is there anything else I should know about her, señor?'

'She'll tell you all there is to know soon enough. She never stops talking.'

Montalban smiled. 'A diamond with a flaw is worth more than a stone without imperfections.'

Ben looked at him coldly. 'You two should get on well together,' he prophesied.

CHAPTER
TWELVE

BEN HAD left the table and was paying the patron by the bar when Sanna appeared in the doorway. She looked radiant, the joy of wearing a silk dress at last reflected in her glowing eyes and quivering excitement.

Luis Montalban's expression was one of undisguised admiration as he came involuntarily to his feet, but she didn't notice him. Her eyes were on Ben, and she smiled with cheeky confidence while he surveyed her critically.

The grey dress had a fitted bodice secured with tiny buttons from the waist to the high ruffled neck, and there were more buttons on the cuffs of the long sleeves. It was as demure as any dress would ever look on Sanna, but he saw immediately that it was a size too small. The cuffs didn't quite reach her wrists, and the front of the full skirt showed her feet, incongruously clad in rough rope sandals. It dipped to brush the floor at the back, and Ben knew the dress was supposed to be worn over a crinoline cage, flat at the front and full at the back to support the grand sweep of the skirt.

There was no doubt, however, that Sanna was thrilled with herself as she walked towards him, twisting exuberantly this way and that so that the heavy silk rustled. 'Listen! I sound as good as I look,' she exclaimed, 'and you should see how grand I am underneath!'

She bent forward to lift her skirt and Ben said hastily
to the goggling patron, 'The señorita's meal,' and he
disappeared regretfully into the back room as she went
on. 'One petticoat of flannel, the next of cotton and the
top one trimmed with the prettiest lace. The patron's
wife said three were the minimum I should wear and
some ladies wear six at a time. Goodness knows how
they manage, because three feels heavy enough,
but . . .' she sighed blissfully. 'So gorgeously *rich*.'

She glanced up at Ben for his approval and then
hoisted her petticoats even higher. 'And look here. Real
drawers, and trimmed with such lovely lace that I declare I wish I could wear them on the outside.' She
touched her bosom. 'I'm very pretty and respectable up
here, too, because I'm wearing a camisole.'

She swished her petticoats and skirt back into place
and held out the flat paper package she carried. 'I've got
another camisole in here and two more pairs of drawers
and another silk dress. Don't you wish you'd stayed so
you could see all the finery?'

She flung an arm around his neck and hugged him
fiercely. 'I do thank you, Mr Maddox, I truly do, and I
hate to ask for anything else, but all this excitement has given me a fearful appetite. Could we eat
now?'

At that moment the black-clothed woman carried
another tray of food over to the table and set out the
dishes, bobbing a curtsy before hurrying away.

'Did you see that?' Sanna breathed. 'I told you I'd be a
proper lady as soon as I had a silk dress.'

Ben took her arm and led her over to the table. She
looked enquiringly at him when she saw Montalban for
the first time, and he bowed courteously.

'This is Señor Luis Montalban,' Ben said, then, 'Give him your hand, Sanna.'

She extended her hand dubiously and her eyes rounded as he kissed it reverently instead of shaking it.

'I've eaten,' Ben went on. 'Señor Montalban will keep you company while I check on the horses. Señor Montalban, this is Miss Susanna Blakeney.'

Montalban bowed again and held out a chair for her. Sanna glowed with pleasure as she sat down. *Miss Susanna Blakeney!* How grand it sounded, and how wonderful that a silk dress could bring about such a change in her and everybody else. There was only one miracle still to be wrought, and that was for Mr Maddox to fall in love with her.

From the way he had introduced her perhaps she already had, but, if not, she had another trick up her sleeve. She had managed to get into only two of the silk dresses at the store, and she was wearing the plainest. She had recognised the other at once as a special occasion gown, and she was positive he could not hold out once he had seen her in it.

It was a pity about the sandals, of course, but none of the finer shoes had fitted her. She had tried and tried but she couldn't bear the pain of cramped bones after being barefooted most of her life. She had rejected the corsets the patron's wife had tried to lace her into for the same reason, but she'd submitted to having her hair divided into two plaits and wound around her head like a coronet. It made her feel cool and queenly, and Señor Montalban must also have thought so from his respectful attitude.

Sanna listened to him with equal, though rather absent-minded, politeness as she daintily ate her way through a dish of tortillas layered with onions and cheese and swimming in red chilli sauce. By the time she was finishing off the meal with deliciously sweet grapes, she had learned that the *hacienda* was entirely self-supporting and that there were many treasures within its walls, a high proportion of which had been brought from Spain in the seventeenth century.

She was impressed, and would have asked many more questions if she hadn't begun to wonder what was keeping Mr Maddox. Certainly he was fussy about his horses, but he should have been back before now.

'It is a great honour to be in charge of the *hacienda*, especially with the family away most of the time,' Montalban was saying. 'I live in luxury, but it is a lonely luxury, for my wife died childless three years ago.'

Sanna's ready sympathy was aroused. 'Perhaps you should take a new one. You're far from old and it's not natural for a man to spend a lifetime in mourning.' She added reflectively, 'For a woman, maybe, but not a man.'

This was the opening he had been waiting for, and he seized it. 'I have been looking for a woman of beauty to preside over the *hacienda*. Now I dare to hope my search has ended.'

She eyed him uneasily, wondering what all his flowery talk was leading up to and deciding not to stay to find out. She reached down for her package. 'Mr Maddox has been an awful long time. I think I'd better go to meet him.'

Montalban said gently, 'He does not wish you to do that. You will enjoy living at the *hacienda*. I will give you everything you wish and more.'

Shock froze the blood in Sanna's veins, and her voice

seemed to come from a long way off, as she asked, 'What do you mean?'

'He said you needed a safe place. I offered my home and myself. He has gone, leaving you in my care.'

'I . . . don't . . . believe . . . you.' The words came out separately, for her lips felt like ice now and wouldn't move properly. She had the weirdest feeling she was somewhere else, and that it wasn't herself speaking at all. She couldn't come to grips with what was happening. The shock was too unexpected, too deep.

A small frown appeared between Montalban's eyebrows. 'I understood that you knew you couldn't continue to accompany him.'

'He says a lot of things he doesn't mean. He can't mean them. We are like . . . like man and wife.'

'I am willing to overlook the past. You will be truly my wife,' he assured her.

The honour was lost on Sanna. She stared at him blankly. 'I don't want to be your wife. I don't love you. I love him.'

'You are not much more than a child, señorita. You have all the adaptability of the young. You will very soon come to care for me. Only let me take you to the *hacienda*, where you can see how splendidly you will live, how much I have to offer you.'

Sanna clutched her package to her bosom as if in protection against him, and jumped up. 'I don't want anything from you. I want my Mr Maddox!'

She ran out of the door, along the street and round to the back of the store, pulling up short. It was true. He had gone. Only Magpie was there, placidly chomping hay. She saddled him quickly, looping her package over the pommel.

She sensed that she was being watched, and turned quickly. Montalban stood there, his hat in his hand, his eyes sad. 'You cannot pursue a man who doesn't want you. Where is your pride?'

'I'm not ashamed of loving a man,' she replied fiercely. 'I would be ashamed if I stayed with you.'

He sighed, and came forward to help her into the saddle. 'I shall be here if you change your mind.'

Sanna gathered up the reins. 'You mean kindly, and I thank you, but you won't be seeing me again. I'm not the sort of woman who can be passed from one man to another. I know who I belong with.' She rode round him to the main street, then galloped Magpie out of the village.

She followed the course of the creek and it didn't ease her anger and humiliation to discover that Mr Maddox must have been so confident she would stay with Montalban that he hadn't bothered to hurry. 'How could you leave me like that?' she yelled furiously as she got close to him. 'Without a word! Nothing. Just leaving Montalban to tell me I wasn't wanted.'

Ben reined in. 'You've always known that.'

Her lips trembled. 'That's not true. Why buy me silk dresses one minute and give me away the next?'

'We had an arrangement,' he reminded her flatly. 'You stayed with me only until I found somewhere to leave you.'

'Necessity never made a good bargain,' she quoted, her anger flaring.

'You liked the *hacienda*, and Montalban would have married you. You'll never make a better bargain than that. I was doing you a favour.'

'Then don't do me any more—and don't ever ride out

on me again. You made me feel like dirt.'

'Are you giving me orders?' he asked, his voice dangerously quiet.

'Yes . . . No . . . I just want you to stop acting as if I'm of no account at all.'

They glowered at each other, Ben having trouble keeping his own temper. 'Do you enjoy being unreasonable?' he demanded.

'I could ask the same about you,' she countered. 'You can't pass me around like a bit of unwanted baggage. We're right together. You just won't admit it.'

'Look, Sanna, that goat-boy told me that the next place we come to will be San Mari-Luz. After that I'll be dead or on my way home, and I'm not taking you with me. If Kirby wins, you'll be his, and you won't have any choice about it, so go back to Montalban while you've got the chance.'

Her lips set stubbornly. 'I'm staying with you.'

'You're stupid.'

'If that's so, then you're not so smart, because a wise man doesn't bother to reprove a fool.'

'Who the hell am I arguing with, you or Mr Blakeney? That man must have been as big a pain as you are with his damfool sayings.'

'Don't speak ill of Mr Blakeney!' she exclaimed. 'He never tried to dump me anywhere.'

'The Apaches saved him the bother.'

'That's a terrible thing to say. They caught him, too, you know, only they killed him. They didn't hurry over it, either.' She shuddered. 'I don't want to talk about that. I don't want to talk about *anything*.'

'If only I could believe that,' he muttered, tossing her the rein of the pack-horse and riding on.

Sanna rode sullenly behind him. She rarely felt sorry for herself but she did so now, and only when she had plumbed the depths of self-pity did she begin to think coherently about herself and Mr Maddox. Why didn't he prize her when Montalban so obviously did?

She fingered the silk of her dress regretfully. It hadn't worked any miracles, after all, and she no longer felt so confident about the blue one in her package. A thought occurred to her, and she called, 'Would it have made any difference if I'd had time to curl my hair?'

He turned. 'What?'

'Would you have wanted to keep me if my hair had been curly?'

'What's that got to do with it?'

'I've never seen a lady with hair as straight as mine. I thought you might like me better if mine was curly,' she explained.

Ben looked up at the sky as if for help, then said, 'I like you best when you're quiet.'

'Señor Montalban appreciated me,' she grumbled.

'That's what I've been trying to tell you.'

Sanna perceived the trap she had fallen into and relapsed once more into silence. Pretty soon she also perceived that she wasn't doing herself any good by sulking. In a resolute effort to cheer herself up, she began to sing.

Ben heard her and it confirmed his belief that she was shallow, that nothing that happened to her scratched below the surface. He wasn't surprised when she turned to him as eagerly as ever that night. He had come to the conclusion that she was as incapable of holding a grudge as she was of feeling deeply.

The next morning they made a late start because Ben

waited for the light to be good enough to clean his guns. He was just finishing this chore when he looked across at Sanna and frowned. Her hair was neatly braided and pinned round her head, but she was sitting cross-legged, wearing only a long camisole and frilly drawers, and searching along the seams of her grey dress. 'What are you doing?' he asked.

'I don't know what you paid for these clothes, but I hope the fleas came free,' she replied, then added with a cry of glee, 'Got one!'

There was a distinctive crack as she crushed it, and Ben's nose crinkled with disgust. 'Very ladylike,' he said scathingly.

'I shouldn't think scratching is very ladylike, either,' she answered, and triumphantly caught and killed another flea.

'You don't have to enjoy it.'

'It's better than itching.' She raised her head from her task and grinned wickedly at him. 'Don't be so hoity-toity. If I've got them, you must have, too.'

Instantly Ben started to scratch his chest, then his arm. Sanna threw back her head and laughed as he stood up cursing. 'Give me your clothes and I'll go through them when I've finished mine,' she offered.

Ben stripped off, wrapped a towel around his waist, slung his saddle-bags over his shoulder and went to the creek to wash. When he returned, Sanna was dressed and his clothes were waiting in a neat pile. He pulled on his trousers and sat down to put on his socks and boots.

'Everything's as clean as a whistle,' she began chirpily, then broke off to stare at him. He had shaved, and for the first time she saw him without stubble or whiskers. She blinked, thinking that if she hadn't already been in love with him she would surely have fallen for him now.

'You're pretty!' she exclaimed and, when he glowered at her, she gurgled with laughter. She went over and knelt beside him, caressing his smooth chin. 'Well, handsome then, give or take a scar or two. I've always thought you were a fine-looking man, but I never realised how fine.'

Her blatant admiration embarrassed him, and he pushed her away, scowling. Unabashed, she chattered on, 'You're younger than I thought, too. Heavens, Mr Maddox, I reckon you're not much older than I am.'

'I'm a hundred years older.' He stood up and turned away from her to start saddling his horse.

Sanna went after him. 'Kiss me while you're all smooth. I want to know what it feels like.'

He ignored her.

'I'll call you pretty again,' she challenged. 'Pretty, pretty, pretty . . .'

When he turned threateningly towards her she flung her arms around his neck and kissed him swiftly. 'Mmmm . . .' she said, and danced laughingly out of his way to escape retribution.

'I've got me a pretty man,' she warbled provocatively as she went over to Magpie. 'A pr-e-e-tty . . .' That was as far as she got, for he seized her and picked her up in his arms.

Sanna kicked her legs, showing a froth of white petticoats, and shrieked with laughter. He was playing. Her so-serious Mr Maddox was actually playing. Then she realised she was the only one laughing, and that he was carrying her towards the creek.

'No!' she cried and clung to his neck. 'No, not in my silk dress! It's new. New to me, anyway.'

He stopped and looked down at her. Frantically she nuzzled his neck, kissing and cajoling him. 'I'll be good. I won't call you pretty again, not ever. Only don't spoil my lovely dress.'

Her cheeks were flushed, her eyes pleading. She looked more helpless than wanton. Much as he wanted to throw her into the water, he found he hadn't the heart to do it. He put her down abruptly and strode back to the horses.

Sanna let out her breath in a whoosh of relief. That had been close. She shook out and smoothed the crumpled folds of her gown as she followed him. She was suitably chastened and yet all the time she was wondering whether it might not have been worth having her dress ruined to be held in his arms like that just a few seconds longer . . .

CHAPTER
THIRTEEN

SANNA CROSSED her fingers, her eyes large with apprehension as she asked, 'That's it? Oh, Mr Maddox, don't tell me that's it!'

Ben lowered his binoculars and nodded. They were at the edge of a belt of trees looking over an arid, shrub-covered plain towards a hill that pointed like a chubby finger at the cloudless sky. Its round sides prickled with impenetrable thorn bushes, and clustering defensively together on the flat top were the squat houses that made up the village of San Mari-Luz. Only one narrow path cleared of thorn bushes led up to it. It was a natural fortress, exactly as the goat-boy had described when Ben had questioned him. Harry Kirby had chosen his bolt-hole well. Two men could hold it against an army, and it was too much to expect that Kirby had gone to ground alone.

'I've never seen such an unfriendly place,' Sanna whispered. 'Please don't go up there, Mr Maddox. You'll be killed. Forget about Kirby and go home.'

'I wouldn't give him the satisfaction.'

'That's just foolish pride.'

'A man's nothing without it. Neither,' he added caustically because he didn't want to be distracted by pointless arguments, 'is a woman.'

Sanna refused to be snubbed. 'Pride's all right for those who can afford it. I've never been able to. Anyway, I don't see why you should worry what a man like Kirby thinks.'

'I don't. It's what *I* think that counts.'

'Well, if pride's got a twin, I reckon it's arrogance, and you've got plenty of that.'

Ben looked at her. 'A bit of your own philosophy for a change, Sanna?'

'Maybe,' she agreed cautiously. 'What's philosophy?'

He was studying the hill again and didn't answer. Sanna felt too dispirited to press him. She was fighting the familiar sick feeling that engulfed her whenever she was afraid something would happen to him. She said miserably, 'If he's up there, he could kill you before you even saw him.'

'He's up there all right. He's too much of a brute to kill me outright, though. There wouldn't be enough spice in it. He gets his satisfaction from making people suffer. Any other man would have faced me months ago to get it over with. Not Kirby. He had to spin it out, make it last. He wants his pound of flesh in full.'

She shuddered. 'Like Shylock in Shakespeare? Mr Plakeney used to rant on a lot about him. That sort of thing makes my flesh creep when it comes from a book and can't harm anybody. You mustn't talk about it in real life. It's flying in the face of providence, and no good can come of that.'

'To hell with providence. It's Kirby I'm after.'

Sanna crossed herself quickly, and he stared at her. 'You Catholic?'

She shook her head, but answered frankly, 'I'm willing to be anything that will keep us alive.'

One of his rare smiles softened his stern mouth. 'I'll grant you one thing. You're an original.'

'Is that a compliment?' she fished hopefully. 'I don't know what it means.'

'It means you're different from any other female I've ever known.'

Sanna didn't like the sound of that, and she grumbled, 'I wouldn't mind being different if I could persuade you not to ride up that awful hill.'

Ben turned in the saddle and studied the sun. It still had a couple of hours to go before it reached its zenith. 'Kirby won't have everything his own way,' he told her. 'When we ride up that path we'll have the sun behind us. He'll have to full glare of it in his eyes.'

'That doesn't sound much of an advantage to me.'

'I've got a better one.' He looked her over critically, and added, 'You.'

'Me?' Sanna was startled.

'You,' he repeated. 'I want you to put on that blue dress you've got in your pack, loosen your hair and ride ahead of me. Kirby has only one weakness I know of. Beautiful women. When he sees one he has to have her, which means he won't risk harming you. That would come later, after he's tired of you.'

His expressionless voice made it all seem very mundane. She stared at him speechlessly, while he went on, 'I've been after him so long I've got to know him as well as I know myself. I'm banking on his lust spoiling whatever trap he's set. You'll be the shield that will get me close enough to him to have a chance.'

'J-just a chance?' she faltered.

'That's all I need.'

Sanna wished she could be as confident as he was, but

she had never heard a more hair-raising scheme in her life and her fear for him was tying her stomach in painful knots.

Ben looked at her white face and continued, 'You don't have to do it. You can wait here.'

She shook her head and replied bleakly, 'No, I can't. It will be worse waiting for you than being with you.'

Sanna slipped from the saddle, reached for her bundle of clothes and took out the blue dress. She had been saving it for a special occasion. She supposed miserably that there wouldn't be one more special than this.

The dress had a fitted bodice with a low neckline and tiny sleeves that were almost off the shoulder. She stripped down to her camisole and stepped into it. The silk felt cool and luxurious as she pulled up the bodice. The full skirt swished importantly. She felt very sick.

The dress fastened at the back, and she looked round for Ben. He was tying the pack-horse to a tree. 'We'll pick him up when we get back.'

Her eyes were dark pools of worry as she asked, 'What if we don't get back?'

'Then your troubles will just be starting. You'll have to get away from Kirby as best you can.'

Sanna couldn't think that far ahead. Her troubles were here and now with the dreadful fear of losing Ben. Her white face took on a green tinge.

'Are you going to be sick again?' Ben asked, remembering the last time she had thought they were close to Kirby.

She swallowed. She must share his confidence, not demoralise him with her own terror. She raised her head jauntily and grinned. 'In my best dress? Never! I'm just waiting for you to button me up.'

He came behind her, and his fingers were calm and purposeful as he did up the long row of tiny buttons. His nearness affected her as it always did. She wanted to turn and put her arms round him, press herself close against the reassuring warmth and strength of his body, distract him from his purpose, if only for a little while.

She fought off the impulse, not wanting to anger him. Not now. Besides, she knew she was powerless. If he loved her, she might be able to stop him riding up that forbidding hill, but he didn't. The love was still all on her side, for him to take advantage of when it suited him. For the moment she didn't care, just so long as he lived.

Yet she felt a terrible sense of loss when he moved away from her. She wanted to say, 'Don't you want to kiss me? It might be for the last time,' but the words were never spoken. She wasn't bold enough to tempt providence the way he did.

Her fingers shook slightly as she undid her plaits and brushed her hair to shining smoothness. She summoned up a cheeky smile. 'You called me beautiful just now. The first time ever. Well, am I?'

'The way you're always on about it, you don't need to be told.' He climbed into his saddle and looked down at her. 'Ready?'

'I suppose so, but I do need to be told. If the way I look is going to keep us alive, I need to be told and told and told!'

'All right, you're beautiful.'

She raised her face. 'Enough to be kissed?'

'There's no time to play around.'

'When is there with you?' she asked wistfully, leaving her belongings by the pack-horse and picking up her shawl and hat.

'You won't need those,' he said as she settled herself into Magpie's saddle. 'Kirby will have binoculars. I want him to get a good look at you.'

'No shawl and hat?' she exclaimed, as if this were the most outrageous thing he had asked of her. 'I'll burn!'

'You won't be in the sun long enough.'

'Then I'll freckle.'

'My God, Sanna, your mind is a mass of trivialities.'

'Freckles aren't trivial. Not to me. A fine lady I'll be, all covered in blotches. I'll look like an egg that doesn't know whether to be white or brown.'

'No shawl and no hat,' he reiterated. 'I'm not having your vanity spoil a good plan.'

'Oh, the plan. You worked it all out without consulting me, as usual. Since I'm risking my neck for you, you might have said something before now.'

'There's not much risk if you do as you're told. You ride ahead of me up the path and into the village. Don't be in a hurry about anything. Kirby's nerves will be strung out. I don't want him to panic. When I tell you to get down, you throw yourself out of the saddle and stay down. Got that?'

Sanna nodded. She hoped it would be as easy as he made it sound. She reminded herself that he was a cautious man. He must know what he was doing, yet loving him so made her so terribly scared. She looped her hat and shawl over the pommel. 'So I can cover up when we come back,' she explained.

He leaned forward, lifted a thick lock of hair from her back and draped it over her shoulder so that it fell over her bosom to her waist. 'Lift your skirt a bit so your petticoats show. A man finds that tempting.'

'You never told me that before,' she said as she obeyed him. 'I'll take my whole dress off if that will help.'

'There's such a thing as being too obvious.' Ben slid his rifle out of the scabbard and nodded to her.

Sanna rode out of the trees and he followed directly behind her. She felt the heat of the sun immediately on her bare arms and hair, but she straightened her back and lifted her head so that she could be clearly seen by anyone watching from that forbidding hill. Soon she was covered in perspiration, and the dust raised by Magpie's hoofs clung to her. Her heart pounded, but the nausea had left her. She had a part to play and she concentrated her whole being on doing it well.

She reached the narrow path through the vicious thorn bushes without anything happening. She began to hope that Kirby had lost his nerve and fled.

The climb was a steep one and a slight breeze Sanna had scarcely been aware of lifted her skirt and snagged it on a bush. It tore as she pulled it free. A little further on a bird rose with a sudden cry of warning. Sanna jumped, and the normally placid Magpie reared.

As she fought to bring him under control on the sharp incline and in the confined space, the spectre of Kirby lessened before the more immediate danger of being thrown on to the cruel thorns. She could hear Ben having a similar battle behind her, and knew the horses had been affected by the tension of their riders.

By the time Magpie had subsided, quivering and snorting, Sanna's dress had been torn in several places.

'You're doing fine,' Ben said behind her. 'Just keep on going.'

'Do you think he's watching us?' she asked, staring

upwards but unable to see anything except bushes and then the sky.

'Don't think about that. Just concentrate on remembering what I told you.'

She rode on, her nerves at breaking-point when she reached the top. A wide dusty street stretched straight ahead of her, edged by rundown houses, some with lean-tos to shade them from the sun, others that must be sweltering ovens behind the closed doors and shutters. At the far end of the street, squat and crumbling, was a church that looked as neglected as the rest of the village. Nothing stirred anywhere, not even a dog. It was not siesta time yet, but the place looked abandoned.

But Sanna felt watching eyes, and she was almost deafened by the tumultuous pounding of her heart. She rode slowly on, knowing Ben was close behind her, listening for his instructions, listening for anything. The tension was too fierce to endure much longer.

A shutter slammed shut, so close and loud that it sounded like a shot. It had the effect of one. Magpie reared again with a shrill whinny and skittered across the street as she struggled to stay in front of Ben. Simultaneously his horse shied and Sanna screamed as a rifle added its explosive crack to the confusion. She looked round to see Ben jerk from his saddle and fall face down in the dust.

There was more screaming. She didn't realise it came from her as she threw herself from the saddle and ran towards him. The horses galloped in panic towards the church. Sanna tripped on her long skirts and covered the rest of the distance to Ben on her knees.

She saw blood flowing from his shoulder close to his neck, and tried to stem it with her fingers, her screams subsiding into whimpers of dread. 'Oh, no!' she said pleadingly. 'No, no . . . .'

'Get away from me,' Ben whispered, unmoving. 'Kirby's on the roof of that church.'

She froze with shock, then tears poured down her cheeks. Through them she saw that, for all the blood, the wound was only superficial. The bullet had made a furrow in the muscle of his shoulder before speeding on its way. 'I thought you were dead,' she murmured. 'I thought . . .'

'I'm trying to fool Kirby, I am,' he hissed. 'Get out of the way before you get us both killed.'

He might have saved his breath. She put her other hand over the wound and rose slowly, both bloody palms held upwards to the sky, shrieking as though she were in agony.

Ben, unable to move without provoking Kirby to fire again, thought she had gone mad. He was sure of it when she fell on her knees beside him and began to writhe and wail, catching up handfuls of dust and throwing them into the air.

CHAPTER
FOURTEEN

HE CLOSED his eyes as the dust came down, fighting the urge to sneeze, and then he understood what she was doing. She was mourning him in Apache fashion to fool Kirby that he was indeed dead. She sounded demented enough to pull it off, and suddenly his position didn't seem so desperate.

Ben opened his eyes cautiously. Sanna was screening him from the church. His rifle lay under his outflung arm and he moved it imperceptibly closer as he asked, 'Can you see him?'

She swayed her body and rolled her head, saying between agonised wails, 'There's a man coming from the side of the church. He's as big as you are but much heavier, as if he's on the way to being fat.' She issued more laments until he got closer, then added, 'He's American. Black hair and black curly beard.'

'That's him,' Ben breathed.

'He's on the left side of the street. He's stopped under a lean-to. Now he's sheltering in a doorway. Mr Maddox, I'm not sure he's fooled.'

She took her knife from her belt, raised her arms in the air and began to slash one of them as she had seen Indian women do in a frenzy of grief. It worked. Kirby moved out of the doorway and, rifle held ready, came towards them.

'Now,' Sanna whispered and threw herself flat.

She pressed her face into the dust and screwed her eyes shut, flinching as Ben fired across her. Then it was quiet, unbelievably quiet.

'Mr Maddox,' she whimpered, afraid to look at him.

She almost collapsed with relief when she felt his hand on her shoulder. 'Stay down until I tell you it's safe,' he ordered.

'He might be fooling, too,' Sanna cried in panic, as he got up and made a crouching run towards Kirby, who was spread-eagled in the dust, his rifle a few feet away from him.

She was quivering with reaction, emotionally and physically spent. She wanted to crawl into Ben's arms and stay there to reassure herself that it was over and that he was safe. The need was so great that she rose shakily to her feet and followed him.

Ben knelt beside Kirby. He had died instantly from a bullet through the heart, a mercy he rarely allowed others. His face was fleshier than Ben remembered, but still handsome, and there seemed a strange defiance in the way his bushy beard pointed towards the sky. He looked as uncompromising in death as he had in life. He hadn't had time to appreciate the irony of falling victim to his own trap.

Ben felt no triumph, only weariness, and something else, too—an awareness that in the last few minutes he had been more afraid than he had ever been in his life. He knew the reason. Sanna. He turned on her angrily as she came up to him. 'I told you to stay put until I said it was safe.'

'I want . . . I need . . .' she began tremulously, but his

eyes were searching the shuttered houses as if expecting Kirby's men to avenge their leader. He couldn't quite believe that a straight duel had ended a vendetta started so many bitter years before.

They both turned at a flutter of movement. A tiny old woman holding a young boy by the hand came hurrying towards them. She was dressed all in black and wrapped in a shroud-like shawl. She walked straight up to Kirby's body and spat on him.

Then she turned to Ben, saw the wariness in his eyes, and said in high-pitched staccato Spanish, 'It was I who banged the shutter to warn you. You have no more enemies here. You have rid us of an evil man.'

'What about his friends?'

The old woman spat again. 'Such a man has no friends, only men attracted to him by greed. The two he came here with fled three nights ago while he slept. They knew you were coming, and they feared you more than they feared Kirby. They called you his ghost, never far behind him. They said you have followed him over deserts and mountains, and through all the seasons, on a matter of family honour.'

She paused, looked down at the corpse, and said with gleaming-eyed satisfaction, 'Well, it is settled now, and so also is the question of my family honour. This man first came here three years ago. He killed my daughter's husband and took her for his woman. Then he went away. Last year he did not come and we thought our prayers for his death had been answered. Then a week ago he reappeared and once more took my Mariquita to his bed, and left me with Damaso, the son from her marriage. That is why I warned you, señor.'

She looked down at the boy. 'Go, Damaso, and tell

your mother it is safe to come home now.' As the boy ran off, she stared venomously down at Kirby. 'The men of this village should have killed each other for the honour of killing him, but there are no men in this village. Only chickens.'

She stared around the street, her black eyes bright, her thin face animated. Ben looked round, too. Silently, almost surreptitiously, men, women and children had come out of their houses. They stared at Kirby from a respectful distance.

'Chickens!' the old lady repeated. She bent her arms and flapped them like wings, running towards the crowd, clucking like a chicken and shouting, 'All hens. Not a cock among them.'

'She's crazy,' Sanna whispered.

'Not as crazy as you are. You just don't know how to do as you're told, do you?' Ben snapped.

'If I did, you might be dead by now,' Sanna flared. She wanted to be comforted, not scorned.

'You don't have to remind me what I owe you. I no sooner settle one score than I'm landed with another.' He glanced down at Kirby. 'I've settled his. I'll settle yours by marrying you.'

Sanna gasped. With outrage, not pleasure. If she had managed to kindle any real feeling within him he wouldn't be talking of owing her anything. Where there was love, there was no debt. Ignorant as she was, she knew that instinctively, and so must he.

Bleakly she remembered a time when she would have married him on any terms. What a child she had been! She was a woman now. She wasn't going to spend the rest of her life being pathetically grateful to him and receiving nothing but scorn in return.

How mad she had been to believe that her love could be enough for both of them. How besotted! How incredibly stupid—for who knew better than she the misery of living in subjugation, unappreciated and unloved? It was to escape that fate that she had run after him in the first place.

Her fury was doused by a suffocating sadness as she wretchedly accepted that, no matter how much she loved him, she could not make him love her in return. There was no love in him. Not for her, anyway.

His begrudging proposal became her final humiliation, and it went deep enough to release her long-suppressed pride. Her back straightened, her chin lifted. 'No, thank you, Mr Maddox. To marry you *I'd* have to owe *you* a great deal and, frankly, I don't feel that I do.'

'Don't talk any more rubbish than you can help,' Ben replied caustically.

Sanna slapped him. She caught him unprepared, and the sound of the stinging blow echoed across the street. The old lady stopped maliciously mocking the men of the village and came scurrying back to them, all smiles and sprightliness now that her venom had been released on her cowering neighbours.

'So . . . so,' she clucked, still very much like the irate chicken she had been imitating. 'You have had so little of fighting today that you must now fight each other? Ah, the excitement of being young.' She chuckled wickedly. 'I am not so shrivelled that I cannot remember. What withers in the body lives on in the mind. But come with me. You have done me a great service, and my house is your house. There you can rest and refresh yourselves while I attend to your wounds. Come, come!'

Ben didn't stir. He was staring at Sanna as if he had

never seen her before. He had the peculiar feeling that the world was rocking and nothing would stay still long enough for him to get his bearings. More than that, he was unable to think clearly. The old lady's words scarcely penetrated his paralysed brain. He said vaguely, 'The horses . . .'

'I suppose you want me to round them up?' Sanna snapped. 'Well, I won't. I'm hot and I'm tired and . . . and my beautiful dress is spoiled.' Strangely, she wasn't worried that the blue silk was torn and bloodstained, but she couldn't tell him what was really wrong with her— that her heart was breaking and she couldn't bear the pain of it.

'What is this?' the old lady asked, her bright black eyes looking from one to the other because they were speaking in English and she couldn't understand.

'I have to get my horses,' Ben explained, switching to Spanish.

'That is not a task for you,' she replied, shocked, then shrilled at a man in the crowd, 'Rafael, get this gentleman's horses, and feed and water them well. The rest of you, remove this carrion meat from the street.'

She kicked Kirby's corpse, took Ben and Sanna by the arm and propelled them towards her house. They ducked under the low doorway and it was immediately obvious how the old lady earned her living. The long narrow room was filled with woven baskets.

She swept an unfinished basket from the table and indicated the chairs. 'Seat yourselves. I shall not be a moment.' She disappeared behind the curtain screening the other rooms in the house.

Sanna and Ben sat stiffly on opposite sides of the table, the silence between them so heavy that it oppressed them both. Sanna's head began to ache. The skin on her face felt so taut she was sure she was smothered in freckles. That didn't seem to matter any more, either. Like Ben, all the familiar touchstones of her life had blurred to insignificance and she was gripped by a weird air of unreality.

Ben said at last, 'I haven't thanked you for what you did.'

He sounded uncertain of himself and that was so strange, too, that Sanna replied swiftly, 'You don't have to. I didn't want Kirby to get his hands on me, that's all.'

The old lady came bustling back. She placed steaming mugs of misela, hot spiced brandy, in front of them. 'In all the excitement I forgot to tell you that I am Señora Rojas. Soon my daughter Mariquita will be here to thank you for what you have done for us.'

She left them again and reappeared with a bowl of hot water and bandages. 'Drink, drink,' she urged Sanna, as she took her arm and studied the self-inflicted wounds. 'You cut well,' she went on admiringly. 'No deeper than the skin. You will heal quickly.'

Sanna sipped the brandy, and her aching head began to spin as her arm was bathed and bound. Surreptitiously she watched as Ben stripped off his shirt and Señora Rojas attended to his wound. It was in an awkward place and she had to wind the bandage under his arm and across his chest to secure it properly.

How terribly close he had been to death, Sanna thought, and shuddered.

'Are you all right?' he asked.

She was so unused to him showing any concern for her that she was instantly on the defensive. 'I'm fine,' she lied, avoiding his eyes and taking another sip of brandy.

There was a slight stir at the open doorway and the boy, Damaso, came in with a woman in her early twenties. She was small and slender and her rather plain face was made beautiful by large slanting brown eyes. They were nothing like Sanna's, but as Ben looked into them, he was curiously reminded of hers. He couldn't think why.

'Ah, Mariquita! Give your thanks to the gentleman who has released you from that defiling monster,' Señora Rojas ordered.

Ben, remembering his sister, stiffened warily as Mariquita came towards him. She was carrying saddle-bags. She put them on the table, seized his hand and kissed it, then retreated hastily to the far end of the room.

'Don't be foolish, Mariquita,' her mother chided. 'You have nothing to fear. This gentleman has his own woman. Would I have told you to come home if it had not been safe?'

Mariquita found her voice and said, her voice as soft as her mother's was shrill, 'Those bags before you were . . . his. They are yours now.'

Ben relaxed. He opened the bags and tipped the contents on the table. Among gold and silver coins, both American and Mexican, were various items of jewellery. He recognised none of it. 'Do you want any of this?' he asked Sanna. 'You've earned it.'

She shook her head fiercely. 'You don't have to buy me off,' she told him angrily.

'I'm not trying to!'

'Well, I don't want it, anyway.'

She was expecting another quarrel, but he just refilled the bags and held them out to Mariquita. 'Take them.

They're as much yours as anybody's.'

Mariquita hung back as if afraid of what taking them might involve. Señora Rojas had no such doubts. She grabbed the bags and hurried into the back room. When she returned, she also seized his hand and kissed it. 'With such a dowry my daughter's shame will be forgotten. Men who scorned her will clamour to marry her. Women who turned away from her will be glad if she marries into their families. Ha! We shall be too fussy, I think. Maybe we shall leave this place of pestilence and go to Mexico City. What do you say, my daughter?'

Mariquita fell to her knees, clasped her hands and looked up at Ben as if he were a saint. 'I have no words . . .' she began.

'You don't need any.' Ben went over and lifted her to her feet, and Sanna, seeing the adoration with which Mariquita looked at him, suffered an excruciating pang of jealousy. When, she thought bitterly, had he ever been half so gentle with her? She might lack the Mexican girl's fragility, but looking big and strong didn't mean she always felt it. Inside, she often felt fragile. He lacked the perception to sense it.

'I shall go to the church and give my thanks to the saints,' Mariquita was saying softly. 'I can always find the words to tell them how I feel.' She took her son by the hand and went quietly out.

Señora Rojas chuckled. 'Damaso will not be doing much praying, I think. Soon he will be running to his friends and telling them of his mother's good fortune. That is as it should be. It is a long time since this family has had anything to crow about, and I mean to crow mightily. Now, I can get you some food?'

'No thanks,' Ben and Sanna said together, then stared

at each other, for neither had ever heard the other refuse food.

'You are not leaving already?' Señora Rojas exclaimed.

'Yes,' Ben said.

'No,' Sanna contradicted.

Ben frowned and switched to English. 'I never stay where there's been trouble. Strike and move on—it's a cavalryman's instinct.'

'I'm not a cavalryman,' she retorted mutinously. 'And my head aches. All my instincts tell me to lie down while I've got the chance.'

'We'll be heading north. Home.'

'I don't have a home.'

'You will when you marry me.'

'I shall never marry you!' she shouted.

'Listen to what you're turning down first,' he shouted back. 'My home is a *hacienda* just like the one we passed the other day. It's . . .'

'I don't care what it is. After all the things you've said about me being an outcast and everything, I don't know why I'm suddenly good enough to marry . . . but I do know you're not good enough for me. I don't want anybody marrying me as a . . . a . . . favour! I'm tired of being cheap. I want to be valued for myself. The man I marry will be proud of me just as I am, no matter what I do or say. I'm not spending the rest of my life having you look down your proud nose at me, Mr High-and-Mighty Maddox.'

'Ben,' he said suddenly. 'My name is Ben.'

'Oh!' Sanna's throat constricted painfully. Her heart felt as though it were breaking all over again. How she had yearned to know his first name. How fiendish of him to tell her now, when she needed to be strong and resolute! Ben . . . She would have given anything to be able to say it aloud. She would have given even more to be able to fling herself into his arms and sob that she had been talking nonsense and didn't mean a word of it. But she couldn't. She was fighting for her own survival as a person. If she crumbled, then no matter how fine a lady she might become in the future, she would always feel worthless inside.

She said at last, 'I've got along fine so far with Mr Maddox. This is no time to change.'

'Exactly what are you sulking about?' he demanded.

'Sulking?' she mocked. 'I'm sparing you the embarrassment of having me for a wife. Remember how you were saying I'd never be accepted by real ladies?'

'There's a way round that. We're not Catholics, but I'll bribe or bully a priest to marry us this side of the border, and take you home as my wife to stop any gossip before it gets started. We'll say you were captured as a young child by Indians and bought from them by a Mexican couple who raised you as their own daughter until I came along and married you. It's close to the truth, and it will make you respectable.'

Yesterday Sanna would have squealed with joy and hugged him to death. Today she merely said coldly, 'And all because you feel you owe me something? You don't, but if it will make you feel better you can take me over the border. That's what I wanted originally, and that's enough. The fact is, Mr Maddox, that I've always felt respectable, and I aim to stay that way. Only if I married you would I begin to feel as cheap as you've always treated me.'

Ben's chair scraped back over the hard-packed mud

floor as he stood up angrily. 'Suit yourself, though when you sober up you'll be changing your tune soon enough.'

Sanna looked down at the empty mug. The brandy had nothing to do with it. It had only given her the courage to say what must have been on her mind for a long time, certainly since he had tried to leave her with Montalban. Now it was said, but she found herself wishing with passionate intensity that she was still naïve enough to believe that her love would make everything right between them.

Ben moved to the doorway, stopped and looked back. 'Are you coming?'

She shook her head, making it ache abominably. 'No. I need to rest.'

'I told you I'm not hanging around here.'

'Then go.' She was too spent to argue any more.

Ben considered her carefully. She did look ill. 'An hour, then. No more.'

It was a concession, and he didn't usually make any. She should have been grateful. She wasn't, yet she could hardly believe it was her own voice replying, 'Don't worry. If you're gone before I wake up, I won't come running after you. I'm finished with all that.'

She propped her elbows on the table and dropped her chin in her hands. She could feel him staring, but she wouldn't look at him. He might read something in her eyes that belied her defiant words. She sensed rather than heard him leave.

Señora Rojas hadn't understood anything they'd said, but she didn't need an interpreter to know they had quarrelled. She said admiringly, 'A man who shouts at a woman, yet doesn't strike her, is a good man. Very rare. You are lucky, señorita.'

Sanna's shoulders shook with laughter. It was the painful silent laughter of unbearable sadness and it bordered on hysteria. Lucky! That was the devil's own jest . . .

CHAPTER
FIFTEEN

SANNA'S WORDS rang in Ben's ears as he strode along the street. '. . . *I won't come running after you. I'm finished with all that.*' No more than she could he believe she'd actually said them. Hadn't he always likened her to ivy, clinging tenaciously to him no matter what he did to dislodge her?

She must have spoken in a fit of pique, but her sulks never lasted long. She would recant soon enough. He didn't know why it was important for him to believe that, which disturbed him deeply.

He had never wanted her with him. The great shadow Harry Kirby had cast over his life was vanquished. She was the only complication remaining. He had repaid her extraordinary courage by offering to marry her. Her refusal had freed him of every tie.

So why did he feel angry instead of relieved? Ben grimly supposed that, much as he had fought against it, he felt responsible for her. Perhaps even guilty.

He frowned and tried to consider her dispassionately. It was difficult. She was such a vital person. Her image in his mind refused to diminish and pale into a problem that could be tackled and solved like any other.

Yet the solution was easy enough. He could take her over the border, give her plenty of money and put her on a stage east, thus ending this violent chapter of his life. Then he could go home and live like any other sane free man, raising crops and cattle and horses, and bothering nobody unless they bothered him.

This prospect, which such a short time ago had been the sum total of all he desired, was suddenly bleak. It was like a well-known picture that had become strangely out of focus, as if something of higher priority had superseded it.

Frowning grimly over this complication to what had been a single burning ambition, to finish the vendetta and go home, Ben found himself at the church which blocked the end of the street. He looked in the open doorway at a scene of slow decay which did nothing to lift his spirits. Rough adobe bricks showed where large chunks of plaster were missing from the walls. The crude thatched roof was no longer weatherproof, and rain had rusted a metal crucifix so that the wall below it was stained like blood.

A figure knelt before the table that served as an altar and a candle burned among many stubs. He recognised Mariquita, and wondered how she could find comfort in such a place. There was none for him. He was about to move away when she turned and looked at him. She smiled. He smiled in return and as he backed out of the doorway he saw her resume her praying.

Ben walked round the side of the church trying to pinpoint what it was about Mariquita's slanting brown eyes that reminded him of Sanna's guileless blue ones, and suddenly he got it. It was the expression. Sometimes he had seen the haunting sadness, with which Mariquita looked at the world, appear in Sanna's eyes. Only occasionally and never for long, yet he felt a strange stirring of pain at the thought that the expression might one day also characterise her.

He told himself that Sanna was too much of a fighter ever to become as downtrodden as Mariquita, but he was more disturbed than ever as he passed the livestock pens behind the church. He wanted—needed—to go on walking, but the flat top of the hill ended in a downward tangle of thorn bushes.

Ben sat down and looked north. Home lay that way. He felt no elation, only this curiously numbing sense of unreality.

To push her from his mind, he visualised the splendour of the forested mountains protectively encircling the rich pastures of Blue Tree Valley, then concentrated on the simple uncluttered beauty of the house itself.

Mentally he roamed from room to room, starting with the great *sala* used for celebrations with its white walls, tiled floor, beamed ceiling and rich dark furniture; then the dining-room with its massive polished table bearing silver and porcelain and crystal, its tall, carved, leather-padded chairs. He wondered whether his father dined there alone or whether he had died. If that were so, then the place at the head of the table would still be set nightly, as was the custom, for the absent master. Himself.

Ben found it a bleak prospect, and his depression deepened. To try to lighten it, his mind roamed on through the family bedrooms, each with its traditional tester bed, beautiful old chests, colourful rugs, corner fireplaces for cold winter nights, and doors and windows opening on to a flower-filled and fountained patio.

He remembered how his stepmother had often sat on the patio outside her bedroom, endlessly embroidering household linen, sharply discouraging the Maddox children from intruding on her bitter broodings of the barrenness of her own body.

It was also there that another cold and collected woman had proposed to him. Linda, the suitable successor to Luisa as mistress of the *hacienda*. It almost seemed to Ben as if they merged into one person. The same rustling silks, the same black hair coiled high to support a large Spanish comb with its filmy mantilla, the same arrogance, the same dignified movements, the same dedication to duty.

So much sameness. Before, he had accepted, welcomed it. Now his reaction was the reverse. He was chilled, revolted. Yet nobody knew better than he the safety of emotional isolation, or that caring too much about anybody made a person vulnerable.

And he had given up being vulnerable. It wasn't compatible with the harsh law of survival he had embraced when, one by one, his softer emotions had withered.

Only now did he realise what a long process that had been. It must have started with his own mother's death and the painful awareness that his stepmother's passion for his father generated no affection for himself or his brothers and sister. Her indifference turned swiftly enough to resentment and even hostility when she had no babies of her own.

If Luisa had laid the foundations of his self-sufficiency, Linda had cemented it when she'd spurned him to get engaged to Gary. The bricks of the wall he'd built around himself had been laid by Gary's subsequent death, and Joseph's. He had been pretty well locked in on himself by the time he'd discovered that ambition and not love had motivated all Linda's actions.

But the final seal, of course, had been applied by his sister, Clare. He'd never had much hope of finding her alive when he set out after Kirby, although the snippets of information he gleaned all spoke of a lovely fair-haired woman riding with the bandit. Then Kirby had discovered who was pursuing him so relentlessly, and his vengeful brutality had once more been triggered off. He'd given Clare to the men who remained with him and left her for Ben to find.

She had been no crushed and pitiful creature, but a raging virago who had turned on him like a wild thing. 'It's all your fault,' she had stormed. 'We fell in love. We were happy until he learned you were after him, then he changed. He punished me to punish you. Why couldn't you leave us alone!'

Clare had always been spirited, but Ben couldn't believe that she and this hysterical, vindictive woman were one and the same person. The change was too great to take in. As she raged on, however, he perceived that his months of hardship following her, Joseph's and Luisa's deaths, and all the misery and destruction the *comancheros* had caused meant nothing to her.

She cared only about Kirby. She was a woman obsessed, incapable of feeling love or loyalty for anybody but him. To prove it she attacked Ben viciously with a knife, believing that, if she killed him, Kirby would be amused or pleased enough to take her back.

Ben had disarmed her after a struggle that had gone on longer than necessary, because he was afraid of hurting her. At that point he had still been unable to comprehend fully that she had changed so completely from the affectionate sister he knew. He put the knife down and gathered her into his arms to comfort her. He might well have tried to embrace a wildcat. She had kicked and clawed and screamed abuse at him.

To give her a chance to calm down, he had backed away, but in her uncontrollable hysteria she had grabbed the knife and stabbed herself. It wasn't a fatal wound. She was young and healthy and she should have recovered. She didn't. For days she lay watching him through hate-filled eyes, bitterly accusing him of ruining her life, and refusing to eat or drink. Finally she died, still hating him as though he, not Kirby, had been her persecutor.

As soon as he was able, Ben telegraphed home the news that she had committed suicide. The true circumstances he would never reveal. It would be thought that she had done the honourable thing. Her memory would remain untarnished to everybody but himself.

The total transference of her allegiance from her family to the man dedicated to destroying it seemed to Ben the ultimate betrayal. No matter how deeply within himself he tried to bury the memory of it, its bitterness remained to sour his soul.

Sitting on the grim hilltop of San Mari-Luz, oblivious to the pitiless sun and the pestering flies, Ben wondered moodily whether it would have given Clare any satisfaction to know she had effectively delivered the *coup de grâce* to whatever remained of his compassion or humanity.

It was she who had added the final shaping to the man he was now, who had confirmed him as a fitting mate for the equally unfeeling Linda and put him beyond the reach of the loving warmth of a girl like Sanna.

'Sanna . . .' Ben said her name aloud and, as he said

it, he realised that all the time they had been together he had been expecting her to commit some act of betrayal. He had been so certain that, sooner or later, she would turn on him that he had actively encouraged her to do so. And she never had. Perhaps that was why she had never seemed quite real to him.

She became very real as Ben realised the enormity of what he had done. He had made her bear the brunt of his past experiences, blamed her for sins she had never committed.

Unable to believe there was such a thing as a loving and loyal woman, he had done his best to crush her. He had ridiculed her finest qualities and mocked her for lacking those which were superficial. She had revered him as some kind of god and he had treated her like an animal. No, his behaviour had been worse than that. He had never been careless with an animal in his life, but Sanna had had to survive as best she could.

And because she had refused to be cowed, and had fought his hostility with uninhibited love and joy and laughter, he had called her stupid. He knew now which of them deserved to be called that. He also knew why his home no longer called to him so urgently. It was because Sanna wouldn't be there.

A feeling of total panic forced Ben to his feet. *Sanna had to be there*. Home would have no meaning otherwise. Nothing would. How could he ever have thought of Linda as a suitable mistress for the *hacienda*? It needed Sanna's warmth and gaiety and sheer joy of living to breathe fresh life into it, just as she had breathed fresh life into him.

Because that's what she had done. Her indomitable spirit, her selfless courage and most of all her capacity for boundless love had broken through the barriers of his emotional isolation. Hadn't she told him once with that quaint homespun wisdom of hers that nobody could go on hating for ever? How foolish he had thought her, and how wrong he had been.

Wrong about so many things. He had wanted her from the moment he had first seen her, but had dismissed it as the physical magnetism of her lovely face and body. Now he supposed he had always loved her or he would never have treated her so harshly. Had he been certain of his invulnerability, he wouldn't have needed to. It was his fear of ever again caring too much for another human being that had impelled him to do his best to drive her away. It was ironic that now, when he knew how desperately he needed to keep her, it seemed he had at last succeeded.

Ben flinched as he thought of the way he had proposed to her. It had been an insult, and she had known it. 'Only if I married you would I begin to feel as cheap as you've always treated me,' she had told him.

Once more he was swamped by panic. Much as he had scorned her when she spoke of love, there was no doubt that she had loved him. What if he had killed it all so completely that there wasn't a spark left for him to rekindle?

The possibility was so real that Ben was gripped by a terrible feeling of helplessness. He would never be able to find the words that might put things right between them. There were no such words, not for him. Much as he might want to go down on his knees and beg forgiveness, he was quite incapable of doing so. He was as much a victim as he had made Sanna of his inability to express his emotions.

But if baring his soul with flowery speech was against his nature, so also was wallowing in helplessness. Ben straightened his back, squared his shoulders and walked purposefully back to the village. He had come to a decision. His floundering were over. He couldn't tell Sanna he loved her. He would have to show her, and hope she understood.

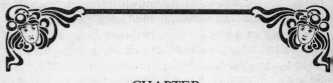

CHAPTER
SIXTEEN

THE DOOR stood open to welcome the cooling breeze. Señora Rojas had anticipated the siesta hour and was fast asleep in a chair. There was no sign of Sanna. Ben walked quietly through the curtain into the back room. There were two narrow beds. Her blue dress was flung across one of them and she lay curled up on the other, wearing only her lace-edged camisole and drawers.

Ben stood looking down at her for a long time thinking how defenceless and vulnerable she looked, and how vulnerable he had himself become because he cared for her so deeply. His eyes roamed from her bandaged arm to her flushed face and he wondered how he could have thought of her as tough and hardy. She seemed frighteningly fragile to him now.

In his new awareness of her importance to him he noticed that although her breasts and hips were as generous as ever, the youthful chubbiness had gone from her face and arms and shoulders. The girl had become a woman before his unappreciative eyes, and the only time he'd told her she was beautiful was when he'd wanted her help in catching Kirby in his own trap.

Ben wanted to lie beside her and hold her close until she felt safe and loved and cherished, but he knew his touch would never make her feel those things. He had taught her too well to expect only lust from him, and the fear that she would misunderstand made him draw back.

The curtain separating the bedroom from the kitchen was pulled aside to allow fresh air from the open back door to circulate, and the breeze ruffled the lace of Sanna's underclothes and stirred a tendril of hair that had fallen across her face.

He took a cover from the other bed and placed it gently over her, resisting the urge to kiss her, for fear of disturbing her. He contented himself with lifting the straying lock of hair from her cheek and then quietly went away.

He left the house, walked along the street and into the store. He recognised the man dozing behind the counter as Rafael, the man Señora Rojas had commanded to care for his horses, and swiftly surveyed the stock. He was surprised how much of it there was for such a poor place, then realised most of it was secondhand and a fair proportion little better than rubbish.

He wanted to buy something pretty for Sanna. This was clearly the wrong place, but there was nowhere else to go. He walked by a rusting stove and a holed tin bath towards the counter, and Rafael sprang to life, rubbing his eyes and bowing.

Damaso had spread the story of how this American was so rich he had given all Kirby's loot to Mariquita, and in his anxiety to profit also, Rafael said eagerly, 'You wish to see your horses, señor? They have been well fed and are now resting in the shade.'

'Later.' Ben thought of the blue dress Sanna prized so much, and which would never be the same again, and asked, 'Do you have any women's dresses?'

'Alas, no. The women of this village make their own.'

'What about a silk cushion?'

Rafael looked as astonished as though Ben had asked for the moon, but he answered quickly 'One could be made. I have a wife and many daughters to sew, and a length of black silk.'

'Haven't you any colours?'

'Not in silk.' Rafael went to a shelf and began moving a few rolls of cloth. 'Perhaps a little white . . . Ah, yes!' He unwrapped a small package of brown paper and produced a piece of white silk. 'It would have to be a small cushion, but it could be made in no time at all.'

Ben nodded and Rafael hurried with the silk into the back room. When he returned he was carrying something wrapped in black cloth. He put it on the counter and unwrapped it carefully. 'If the señor is looking for a present for a brave and beautiful lady . . .' he began winningly.

Ben found himself looking at an ornate, long-handled, silver-backed mirror with a matching hairbrush and comb, and knew that Kirby, or somebody like him, had traded at the store. 'I'll take it. What about a side-saddle?'

He expected another look of astonishment, but Rafael beamed delightedly. 'I have one, señor. It is an old one for it has been here since my father's time, the saints rest his soul, but the leather is beautiful and has been well cared for.'

'Let's see it.' Ben could hardly believe his luck, and neither could Rafael, who also produced a long bearskin cape which would keep Sanna warm on the coldest of mountain nights.

By the time Ben had completed his purchases and checked over his horses the best part of an hour had gone by. He drank coffee with Rafael to kill more time, for his anxiety to leave San Mari-Luz was tempered by his need for Sanna to have all the rest she wanted.

When he returned to the house Damaso was sitting cross-legged on the floor, Señora Rojas was working on a basket and Mariquita was placing freshly made lemonade and mugs on the table. 'You would like some, señor?' she asked shyly. When he shook his head, she went on with a smile, 'The señorita is awake. If you will be seated, she will not be long.'

He had no sooner sat down than Sanna came into the room. He stood up again and she looked at him uncertainly. She supposed he was cross with her for delaying him and impatient to be away.

Ben's hopes that the things she'd said had been no more than a flash of temper died as he studied her set face. There wasn't a hint of the engaging and ready apologies which signalled the end of her sulks. No, she had meant what she'd said. He felt a chill sense of loss for his loving, laughing Sanna. He wanted her back, and she didn't want him at all.

'Have you slept long enough? Do you feel better?' he asked.

Sanna nodded dumbly, his concern taking her by surprise. She didn't trust herself to speak. Her throat was desperately dry but, worse than that, the impact of his physical presence was wreaking its usual havoc on her defences. How weak she was. How stupidly, mindlessly, weak. His depthless blue eyes could still draw the very soul from her, still melt her bones so that she was a quivering mass of yearning. She wondered where she had ever found the will and the words to defy him.

She realised he was holding out a chair for her, and she sat on it in astonishment. When he poured a mug of lemonade and gave it to her courteously, her astonishment turned to disbelief.

'Are you hungry?' he asked.

She shook her head.

'Are you sure you're well enough to ride?'

She nodded again, feeling disoriented. Why was he behaving so strangely? Why wasn't he bad-tempered, the way he always was when he'd lost good riding time?

'We could wait until it's cooler if you like,' he offered.

Sanna was totally unnerved. She snapped. 'Why are you fussing me?'

'I'm not fussing you,' he replied quietly. 'I'm treating you as I should have from the beginning, like the lady you are. I'll fetch the horses while you drink your lemonade.'

She stared speechlessly after him as he left. She would have been far less shocked if he had slapped her. Señora Rojas broke into animated chatter, but none of her words penetrated Sanna's numbed brain. She'd almost convinced herself he was being nice to her because he intended to run out on her again when she realised that he'd scarcely have waited for her to wake up first. But if it wasn't that, what was it?

She was still grappling for a solution to his strange behaviour when the sound of horses being brought to the door sent Señora Rojas into effusive farewells, which also engulfed Ben when he came in.

Ben was carrying Sanna's shawl and hat, and her nerves jumped as he put the shawl round her shoulders. She grabbed the hat and jammed it on her head, almost fleeing out of the door. She stopped short when she saw Magpie, demanding, 'What's that?'

'A side-saddle. The sort ladies use.'

Sanna turned on him furiously. 'If you're angry with me, yell at me the way you usually do. I've known you be a lot of things but never spiteful. We both know I'm not a lady. There's no need to mock me.'

'I'm not mocking you. I'm trying to help you.'

'I don't want your help. It makes me feel funny.'

'It makes me feel better.' When she stared at him uncomprehendingly, he went on, 'You've never been anything but a lady. I'm a bit late admitting it, but I know it now, and I'm going to make damned sure everybody else knows it, too. With or without your co-operation.'

He placed his large hands around her waist and lifted her into the saddle before she could marshal another protest. Her eyes brimmed with indignation as he placed her right knee round the pommel, arranged her skirts and slid her left foot into the stirrup.

'You'll soon adjust,' he told her. 'Keep your back straight, your shoulders and arms relaxed, and leave the rest to Magpie.'

'I feel like a flea on a dog's tail, likely to be flicked off at any moment,' she said stonily, then wished she'd preserved a dignified silence, because he smiled and her perfidious heart somersaulted.

'You'll be all right. I'll keep a close watch on you and we'll camp before you get tired.'

Sanna's throat constricted as he climbed on to his own horse and she brooded darkly on her own capriciousness. Why, if she could be so stoic when he was harsh, should she feel so weak and tearful when he was kind?

She was scarcely conscious of waving goodbye to

Señora Rojas, Mariquita and Damaso as Ben walked his horse along the siesta-quiet street and Magpie followed out of habit. She was beset by one bewildering question after another, but they were temporarily pushed to the back of her mind by the need to concentrate on getting safely down the tortuous path through the thorn bushes without falling from the strange saddle.

No sooner were they on the plain, however, than she burst out, 'Are you being nice to me because I helped you with Kirby?'

'No.'

'Oh.' Sanna looked at him suspiciously. He was riding companionably beside her, instead of ahead as usual, which unsettled her further, if that were possible. She thought again, and tried, 'Because you've had time to reconsider and you're grateful I won't marry you?'

'No.'

'Then you are mocking me,' she burst out, 'and I hate you for it. Do you hear me, Mr Maddox? I hate you!'

It was only the second lie she had ever told him. The first had been to say that she'd helped him with Kirby because she was afraid of falling into the *comancheros'* hands, and she had lied because she couldn't bear him to think he was obliged to marry her. Ben hadn't believed her because he knew her kind of loyalty didn't spring from fear.

But he believed her second desperate lie, because back there in San Mari-Luz he had heaped one humiliation too many on her. He had killed her love at the very moment he had accepted that it was real and selfless. He would never have proposed to her otherwise. There were too many other ways of settling an obligation.

'I'm not mocking you,' he said at last. 'I don't need telling that if there's a fool around here, it's me.'

Sanna bit her lip. 'I can't make any sense of what you're saying, Mr Maddox. I don't understand you any more.'

'I don't suppose you do.' He looked ahead, his eyes bleak. 'It's going to take time.'

'I don't like not understanding things,' she complained. 'It makes me feel peculiar. As if I've missed something somewhere and I don't know what. Unless . . .' She drew in her breath and broke off.

'Unless what?' he prompted.

A slow flush burned up from Sanna's shoulders and scorched her cheeks. 'Unless you're th-thinking about tonight,' she stammered. 'I'll cook and clean the same as always, but I'm not sharing a blanket with you. It was all right while . . . well, it was all right once, but it isn't any more. If you think all this lady business , . .'

'I don't think that.'

The anger in his voice cut through Sanna's confusion and gave her something recognisable to grasp and hang on to. He wasn't so very different. He was just trying to be. Her first solution to his puzzling behaviour must have been the right one. He felt he owed her something, and a gentleman always paid his debts.

Sanna didn't want to be a debt. Her new-found pride rebelled against it, causing her wavering hostility to throw out fresh defensive prickles like a withering cactus responding to a life-giving deluge of rain.

She took refuge in a silence that was so frigid and uncharacteristic that it beat against Ben's ears with an almost physical force. He yearned for her nonsensical chatter, her cheerful whistling or even the off-key wailing she called singing—anything that would reassure him that he hadn't crushed all that was best in her.

He needed her sunny nature to warm his own. He needed . . . Ben checked his thoughts abruptly. He would go mad if he dwelt on all he needed from her.

By the time they entered the trees to recover the pack-horse, Sanna had relaxed sufficiently in the side-saddle to begin to enjoy the feeling of status it gave her. She felt positively queenly perched graciously like this, but she kept her delight to herself, afraid he would think her no better than a child to be won over with a new toy.

When he dismounted she sat frowning at the ground, wondering how she could reach it without becoming entangled in her skirts. Ben solved the problem by plucking her out of the saddle and setting her lightly on her feet.

She turned away quickly, flustered by his touch, her wilful body making a mockery of her determination not to respond to him. She busied herself pulling her plain grey dress from her bundle of clothing and was confronted by a fresh problem. She needed his help with the tiny impossible-to-reach buttons at the back of her blue dress.

She stood irresolute, and Ben paused in his task of loading up the pack-horse. 'My buttons . . .' she said.

She stiffened defensively as he came behind her and began to work on the buttons. Ben needed to summon up his own self-control as the tight bodice parted, to reveal the seductive curve of her back. He was almost down to the waist when she began to tremble. He stopped and laid a soothing hand on her shoulder. 'Relax. I'm not going to take advantage of you.'

Sanna, despising herself for the knowledge that

she would be unable to resist him if he did, snapped defiantly, 'Of course not. It's the wrong time of day.'

Ben sighed, and went to work again on the buttons. 'Now who is being spiteful, Susanna?'

She whirled away from him, clutching her bodice to stop it falling from her shoulders. 'Don't call me that!'

'It's what you've always wanted,' he pointed out.

'I don't want any favours from you!' Sanna stamped her foot to reinforce her point and had to make another wild clutch at her bodice.

She expected him to shout back at her the way he always did, but, after considering her for a long moment, he said calmly, 'I think you'd better get yourself properly clothed. I'm not made of iron.'

Sanna blushed and fled through the trees, aware she was being idiotically prudish. They had been lovers for long enough, for heaven's sake, and here she was behaving as though he'd never seen her naked flesh. She knew she wasn't, and never could be, afraid of him. It was herself she distrusted. He had only to look at her in a certain way and her body responded with the abandon of a barnyard cat. It was a problem she had been unaware of when she'd set out to become a lady.

The demureness of the grey dress with its long sleeves and high collar enabled her to return with a semblance of dignity. She was passive when he lifted her into the saddle, but swiftly arranged her legs herself this time. She loosened the lace on her hat and felt more in control when her face was veiled from him.

'I've got the hang of this saddle, but I don't know if I'm ready to cope with the pack-horse yet,' she told him.

'That will be my job in future.' He got on to his horse and began to lead the other one through the trees.

'I don't know about that,' she argued as she followed him. 'I feel safer when you're in front with your hands free.'

'I managed well enough before you joined up with me,' he reminded her, 'so you can stop worrying. I'm not going to let anything happen to you.'

Perversely, the lifting of responsibility from her shoulders aggrieved rather than pleased Sanna. It was like the side-saddle. The joy was spoilt because he was treating her like a lady not from inclination, but from the need to settle what he saw as a debt.

He set an easy pace and rode beside her, and several times she had to stifle the urge to talk. Keeping her thoughts and emotions suppressed was so unnatural to her that she surprised them both when she suddenly burst out, 'What's it short for?'

'What?'

'Ben.'

The question came so much out of the blue that he was too surprised to answer for a moment.

'Is it Benjamin?' she persisted.

'No. Benedict.' When she smothered a sound that seemed suspiciously like a chuckle, he added, 'It's all right. I don't like it, either.'

'It's just that it sounds so . . . so saintly,' she replied, and began to giggle helplessly.

The tight knot of pain within him eased a fraction. The real Sanna was still very much alive, there to be reached if only he could find the right way. She had shut him out, but there was no barrier strong enough to contain her natural exuberance for long. It was too much to expect her love for him to return with her laughter, and yet he hoped it would for no reason other than that he had to.

Sanna, knowing how he hated to be teased, sneaked a mischievous glance at him. She was taken aback when she saw that, instead of scowling, he was smiling. Her heart fluttered, causing her relaxed nerves to tighten into tingling alarm. She was on the verge of sacrificing her pride and integrity for the price of a single smile! The laughter died from her eyes and she retreated once more into the safety of silence.

Ben found a fine campsite a good two hours before sunset. It was in a rock-strewn hollow screened by bushes and trees. There was firewood to be gathered and a meal to be cooked, but Sanna could summon up none of her usual enthusiasm for setting up camp or even for food. She stirred a fallen log with her foot and, when nothing ran from underneath it, sat down and took off her hat.

She watched Ben unsaddle the horses and unload the pack-horse, looking away whenever he glanced at her, as if meeting his eyes was a forbidden intimacy.

She felt more vulnerable than the first time they'd camped together. Her fear that night had been physical, and conquerable, but now it was emotional and infinitely worse. Every time she thought she was in control of herself he could so quickly prove her wrong. And so she watched him covertly, waiting for she knew not what, but waiting all the same . . .

CHAPTER
SEVENTEEN

SANNA WASN'T the only one floundering in a sea of
uncertainties. Ben was a decisive man. If something
needed to be done, he did it, yet he was finding it
extraordinarily difficult to give Sanna the presents he
had bought her. He had never been a ladies' man and
would have found courting in the conventional way
difficult enough, but to woo a girl who was his wife in
everything but name crippled him with embarrassment.

His predicament wasn't helped by the fact that he
could not justify himself by telling Sanna about his
sister's treachery, and how in some way he had expected
the same behaviour from her. Clare was a closed book,
and family loyalty dictated that he could never reveal the
sordid details of the final chapter of her life, even to win
the woman he loved.

Besides, he was no longer seeing everything in black
and white, clear and indisputable. His love for Sanna
had merged several incidents in his life to grey, among
them those last days with Clare. He understood her
more, for her commitment to the man she loved didn't
seem so very different from Sanna's commitment to
himself during the duel at San Mari-Luz.

But his reawakened compassion highlighted rather
than disguised the main difference between the two

women. Clare's love had made her readily corruptible; Sanna's had been as fierce without affecting her integrity. She hadn't sold her soul to the man she had been willing to die for, even at the price of gaining everything she had ever dreamed of.

Ben fidgeted around the camp, suffering the double ache of loving and being incapable of expressing his love, until despair at his own ineptitude made him stride towards her and dump the parcels in her lap with a desperation that was close to a challenge.

He saw her jump and retreated across the camp, the words he had painfully framed to accompany the presents lost in his bungling confusion. He sat down on a boulder and made a great show of being engrossed in checking his guns.

Sanna's confusion was scarcely less than his own, and the parcels slipped from her lap. She retrieved the largest one, and asked, 'What's this?'

'Some things you need.' He sounded surly, as if defying her to argue.

Sanna sat quite still then, hesitantly, almost afraid of what it might contain, she unwrapped the parcel. She didn't want any presents from him. She couldn't accept them in the uncomplicated way she had taken the dresses and underwear, never questioning his motives. If there was one thing she could be certain of it was that he never did anything without a purpose, and, not knowing what that purpose was, she was deeply suspicious.

She gasped as her fingers touched fur, and gasped again when she held it up and saw that it was a silk-lined cape, an unbelievable luxury. She was unable to resist holding the fur against her cheek for a precious, self-indulgent moment before suppressing a sigh and putting it aside.

Ben, his head bent over his rifle, was none the less studying her under frowning eyebrows. The old Sanna would have put on the cape and danced across the camp to hug him, her excitement spilling out in words and smiles and tears. Her unnatural silence was one more death-knell to his hopes . . . the hopes that had risen so dramatically with her laughter over his name that afternoon.

Sanna unwrapped the next parcel and stared at the mirror, brush and comb. She had never had any resistance to lovely things. She yearned to pick up the mirror by its beautifully embossed handle and gaze at herself while she brushed her hair, but allowing herself to fondle the fur had almost been her undoing, making it so much harder to put aside. Even so, her wilful fingers strayed towards the mirror and lingered on the silver before she could summon up the resolution to put the dressing set on top of the cape.

She looked at the third parcel and knew she mustn't open it. There wasn't an ounce of resistance left in her. She put it with the others, carried them across the camp and put them beside Ben.

She found the strength to meet the fathomless blue of his eyes, and said with a forthrightness she was far from feeling, 'I believe you meant these kindly, and I thank you, but I can't accept them.'

Ben got slowly to his feet. 'There's nothing to accepting things you need, Susanna.'

'Susanna . . .' she repeated. 'Calling me that is part of it, isn't it? You've fixed it in your head that you're beholden to me and you're trying to pay me back, but don't you see that if I let you, then I'll be beholden to you? There's only one way I can pay you, and that's with my body. You won't be making me into a lady, you'll be making me into a whore.'

Her reasoning struck Ben dumb, enabling her to continue, 'I won't say I haven't been sorely tempted, because I have, and I'd be obliged if you don't tempt me any more. I'm not always as strong as I should be, and it wouldn't be kind of you to trade on that. What it really comes down to, Mr Maddox, is that if you honestly want to do me a service, you'll stop trying to ease your conscience at the expense of mine.'

'How, in the name of all that's wonderful, did you manage to dream up that pack of nonsense?' Ben breathed.

Sanna's chin lifted and a martial glint came into her eyes, her composure shaken by anger. 'You're doing it again, talking as though anything I say is of no account because I'm stupid. Well, it had better not be nonsense, because the alternative is so nasty I don't want to believe it, even of you!'

'Don't stop there. What don't you want to believe?'

'That you got me those pretty things so that I'd carry on sleeping with you, and that's *deliberately* making me into a whore.'

Stung, Ben retorted, 'I don't want to make you into anything, for God's sake, except my wife.'

Sanna's fists clenched. 'Don't say that! I'm not a debt to be settled, like Kirby.'

'I know you're not, but I also know you didn't make all this fuss when I bought you the silk dresses.'

'That was different. No,' she contradicted herself, 'I was different. I didn't see anything wrong in . . . in you and me then. The way we were together.'

Ben drew in his breath, trying to calm himself to retrieve an almost irretrievable situation. It had all gone wrong, and he knew why. He had assumed that Sanna would understand, without any explanations, what he was trying to do, and that was expecting too much. He had never given her any reason to think the best of him, so naturally she thought the worst. Instead of winning her back he had driven her further away, and unless he said the right things, and quickly, she would be lost to him for ever.

The words spun round in his brain, beating against the barrier of his reticence but unable to break it down. All he managed to mumble finally, and that by avoiding her eyes, was, 'There was nothing wrong in the way we were together except . . . except my attitude. That's what I'm trying to put right.'

As an explanation, it was woefully inadequate. He picked up the unopened parcel and placed it in her arms. Sanna tried to give it back. 'I don't want it.'

'Take it,' he said quietly. 'It's something I need you to have. I'm no good with words. Maybe it will tell you all the things I can't.'

Something in his voice, and in the way he wouldn't look at her, stopped her arguing, and she wasn't sure why. She turned the parcel over in her hands. He hadn't said 'something you need' but 'something I need you to have'. She couldn't think what that might be and, while she wondered, she slowly unwrapped the parcel.

The paper slipped from her fingers when she saw what it contained. 'Oh,' she gasped. She turned her back on him, burying her face in the soft white silk and nuzzling it lovingly as though it were a living thing. 'Oh,' she gasped again, and very nearly cried all over it.

Ben was beginning to think he had at last done something right, when she rounded fiercely on him. 'Why did you have to give me this? Why? Because it's the only thing I can't refuse? Or so that I'll know the way you've been treating me all afternoon, calling me Susanna and everything, was just a big joke? This is so I'll be sure to know it, isn't it, because you said yourself that all the silk cushions in the world wouldn't make a lady out of me!'

'Sanna . . .' Ben was so aghast that he slipped unconsciously into her old name.

She swung away from him and began striding up and down the camp. 'Do you know something, Mr Maddox? You're right. Look at me. Do you know what I'm trying to do? I'm trying to throw this cushion down so that I can sit on it, the way ladies do. And I can't. After wanting to for so long, I can't! I'm too scared it will spoil. Isn't that funny? Doesn't it want to make you laugh?'

Her blue eyes blazed into his, but she was trembling, and he had never seen her so distressed. He took a step towards her. She backed away and screamed, 'Don't come near me. Don't you dare come near me.'

Ben stopped. He said quietly, 'If you can't throw it down, I'll do it for you.'

'No!' She backed further away. 'When I dreamed about it, it was always clean. I couldn't bear it to get dirty.'

'If it does, I'll get you another, and another, and when we get home you can have a house full of them.'

'Don't talk about home like that. What if your father's alive? What would he think about me? And what sort of a person would I be if I let you lie to him to protect my name?'

Ben took another cautious step towards her. 'Once he sees you, and certainly when he knows you, no explanations will be necessary. In any case, he wouldn't think much of me if I didn't do everything I could to protect my wife.'

Sanna stamped her foot. 'Don't call me your wife. It's not true, and it never will be. What about the woman who is waiting for you?'

'Waiting was her own idea. I never asked her to.'

'Oh,' Sanna moaned, 'I don't understand anything any more. Not you, or me or anything. Why don't you want her?'

'She doesn't seem good enough any more.'

'But you said she was a lady!'

'I've found a better one.'

'Will you stop mocking me!' she shouted.

'I'm not mocking you.' Ben covered the last of the distance between them and such was his exasperation that he took her by the shoulders and shook her. 'I mean it. I also mean to marry you. I know you've never had a free choice about anything and I'd like to give you one now, but I'm not that noble. You're mine and I'm hanging on to you.'

'Don't say that. You sound as if you c-care about me.'

'Don't keep telling me what I can and can't say. It's taken me long enough to get started.' Ben suddenly realised he was still shaking her, and stopped. 'I'm sorry. I'm still blaming you for things that are not your fault. I'll get out of the habit if you'll give me time. God knows you've every reason to hate me.' He released her and turned away.

'I don't hate you.'

The words were whispered, as if uttered against her will, but he heard them and swung back towards her. 'That's something,' he said wistfully. 'But you did love me. Did I kill it all, Sanna?'

She was the one who avoided his eyes this time. She looked down at the cushion, and her fingers dug into it as she replied, 'I promised myself something back there in San Mari-Luz. I promised I would never give you any reason to scorn me again. Well, if I married you I'd have to tell you things about myself you don't know. Things I didn't think were important until you showed me how ignorant I was about what ladies are really like.'

Ben came closer to her and looked down at her bowed head. She had always seemed so uncomplicated, and it shattered him to realise he knew as little about what was going on in her mind as she knew about his. He put his hand under her chin and gently raised her face. 'There's nothing you could tell me that would stop me wanting to marry you.'

Sanna bit her lip. She wanted to believe him. She wanted to believe so much that the impossible had happened and that he had fallen in love with her. For a delirious moment hope and happiness surged through her before being overcome by her doubts and fears. Then she said wretchedly, knowing she would invoke the scorn she dreaded, 'I can't read or write.'

She stiffened her spine and lifted her chin defiantly. It was out. He could laugh or mock, but at least he would know, as she had come to know so painfully, what an impossible pair they were.

'I never supposed you could,' Ben replied.

Sanna gasped and stuttered: 'B-but I thought you'd despise me.'

'Don't tell me that's why you refused to marry me!' Ben exclaimed, stunned.

'Yes,' she wailed. 'I l-love you so much. At the beginning I th-thought that being beautiful was enough, that you would be proud of me—but then I came to see you c-couldn't be proud of anybody as ignorant as I am. So I became proud. I had to. It hurt so much, you see, not being good enough. Then everything got so muddled. I didn't know what I was doing or saying, only that I was hurting . . .'

'Sanna, my precious idiot,' Ben breathed, reaching for her, then pausing as he corrected himself swiftly, 'I'm sorry. I didn't mean to call you that.'

Her eyes filled with tears. 'I don't mind the "idiot" if the "precious" goes with it. You make it sound loving, as though you really cared for me. You do, don't you?'

Dumbly, unable to believe in his own turn that she cared for him, he nodded.

'Enough to teach me to read and write?' she asked, her tear-drenched eyes fixed intently on his.

'More than enough. It doesn't bother me, but I mean to make sure nothing ever bothers you again.'

Sanna needed no further proof that her proud and impatient Mr Maddox loved her. Her tears finally spilled over and she went unresistingly into his arms. 'Don't cry,' he whispered. 'I can't bear to see you cry.'

'It's because I'm s-so happy,' she wept. She found the silk cushion she was clutching a bar between herself and the sweet comfort of his body. Unthinkingly she threw it away. She pressed her wet face against his neck and nuzzled him in the loving way he'd never expected to experience again. His grip on her tightened and he buried his face in her hair.

For a long while it was enough just to cling to each other, then Sanna said, 'Why didn't you tell me you loved me when you asked me to marry you? Why let me think I was some awful debt that had to be paid off?'

'I still had to admit it to myself,' Ben replied huskily. 'I'd made up my mind a long time ago never to care too much about anybody. It seemed the safest way to . . . to survive. Then I met you, and it didn't work any more. I learned the hard way that I couldn't hurt you without hurting myself twice as much.'

He sighed and pressed her closer. 'By then I thought I'd lost you. I've never been so scared in all my life. I thought I'd never win you back. That's why I'm hanging on to you so tightly. I still can't believe it.'

'You never lost me,' Sanna murmured, raising her hand to trace the outline of his lips. 'Not really. I made a lot of fuss, but I couldn't fight myself and you. I love you too much.'

He kissed her fingers, then bent his head and kissed her lips tenderly, almost reverently, so that she felt their very souls were merging. She gave a shuddering sigh of bliss. 'This is loving, isn't it, Ben? Not lust. True loving.'

'Yes.' He kissed her again and rubbed his cheek against hers in the touching way he had learned from her. As he raised his head, something caught his eye. 'Sanna, your cushion's on the ground.'

'Mm, I know,' she replied dreamily. 'It doesn't matter now. It was only a symbol of what I was reaching out for. So were the silk dresses and the fine white house. I didn't know about love then, so I thought I was yearning for possessions. The gentleman to go with them didn't seem half so important.'

She smiled, her eyes shining mischievously. 'That's your precious idiot for you, Ben. I had everything the wrong way round, as usual. Now I know nothing matters, nothing at all, so long as I have my gentleman.'

He looked conscience-stricken. 'Gentleman! You got a rough deal there.'

'Gentleman,' she repeated firmly, then spoiled her effect with a chuckle. 'A bit reluctant sometimes, maybe, but I'm not likely to complain, since I've never been led to expect too much.'

'You'll have everything you ever dreamed of,' he promised. 'I need to spoil you.'

'Oh, Ben, I've just told you I've got something better than a foolish dream. I've got you.'

'If you'd never dreamed, you'd never have run after me.' He shuddered. 'That doesn't bear thinking about, so if your dream isn't important to you, it's very important to me. That's why I gave you the silk cushion. I was hoping you'd realise I meant to make it come true.'

He crushed her into his arms, kissing her with an intensity that revealed the depths of his feelings as no words could. Her senses swam. She could only marvel that somehow the miracle had happened, and that this harsh and taciturn man had come to love her as passionately as she loved him.

When she could, she said shakily, 'Ben, you know what I was saying about this being truly loving, and not lust? Well, I dare say it's because I'm not a proper lady, but the one's got so mixed up with the other I can't tell the difference right now.'

'Thank God for that,' he breathed. 'I was wondering

how to tell you I've got the same problem. Promise me, Sanna, that when you're sinking under silk cushions and dresses you'll never change. Promise me you'll never be a proper lady.'

'I promise,' she murmured demurely, 'but *Susanna*, please! I mean to keep up appearances.'

Ben laughed, a carefree and joyful sound, and swept her up into his arms.

Mills & Boon

Your chance to step into the past Take 2 Books FREE

Discover a world long vanished. An age of chivalry and intrigue, powerful desires and exotic locations. Read about true love found by soldiers and states-men, princesses and serving girls. All written as only Mills & Boon's top-selling authors know how. Become a regular reader of Mills & Boon Masquerade Historical Romances and enjoy 4 superb, new titles every two months, plus a whole range of special benefits: your very own personal membership card entitles you to a regular free newsletter packed with recipes, competitions, exclusive book offers plus other bargain offers and big cash savings.

AND an Introductory FREE GIFT for YOU. Turn over the page for details.

Fill in and send this coupon back today and we will send you
2 Introductory Historical Romances FREE

At the same time we will reserve a subscription to Mills & Boon Masquerade Historical Romances for you. Every two months you will receive Four new, superb titles delivered direct to your door. You don't pay extra for delivery. Postage and packing is always completely free. There is no obligation or commitment – you only receive books for as long as you want to.

Just fill in and post the coupon today to **MILLS & BOON READER SERVICE, FREEPOST, P.O. BOX 236, CROYDON, SURREY CR9 9EL.**

Please Note:- READERS IN SOUTH AFRICA write to Mills & Boon, Postbag X3010, Randburg 2125, S. Africa.

FREE BOOKS CERTIFICATE

To: Mills & Boon Reader Service, FREEPOST, P.O. Box 236, Croydon, Surrey CR9 9EL.

Please send me, free and without obligation, two Masquerade Historical Romances, and reserve a Reader Service Subscription for me. If I decide to subscribe I shall receive following my free parcel of books, four new Masquerade Historical Romances every two months for £5.00, post and packing free. If I decide not to subscribe, I shall write to you within 10 days. The free books are mine to keep in any case. I understand that I may cancel my subscription at any time simply by writing to you. I am over 18 years of age.

Please write in BLOCK CAPITALS.

Signature _____

Name _____

Address _____

_____ Post code _____

SEND NO MONEY — TAKE NO RISKS.

Please don't forget to include your Postcode.

Remember, postcodes speed delivery. Offer applies in UK only and is not valid to present subscribers. Mills & Boon reserve the right to exercise discretion in granting membership. If price changes are necessary you will be notified.
4M Offer expires December 24th 1984.

E